PRAISE FOR
FLEABRAIN LOVES FRANNY

"Heartwarming and endlessly funny,
Fleabrain Loves Franny will delight readers of all
ages. Rocklin's sharp wit and exuberant writing style
are refreshing. This book is not to be missed."
—*VOYA*

"Franny—a compassionate, thoughtful and
sympathetic protagonist—is believably erratic in her
emotions and reflections on her illness and
its effects on her previously carefree life."
—*Publishers Weekly*

"Rocklin perfectly captures the era of 1952 and
creates a sympathetic, realistic character in Franny,
who begins to accept her condition, rejoin her friends
and even protest her school's inaccessibility."
—*Kirkus Reviews*

"Comedic and philosophical, readers will
find multiple levels to enjoy."
—*School Library Journal*

AMULET BOOKS
NEW YORK

Fleabrain
LOVES
Franny

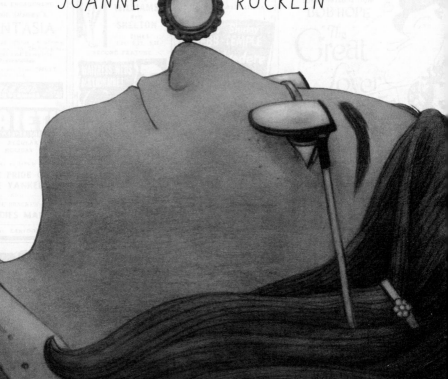

JOANNE ROCKLIN

To my dear friend Arlene Moscovitch, kindred spirit
and book sharer since third grade

PUBLISHER'S NOTE: This is a work of fiction. Names, characters, places, and incidents are either the product of the author's imagination or are used fictitiously, and any resemblance to actual persons, living or dead, business establishments, events, or locales is entirely coincidental.

The Library of Congress has catalogued the hardcover edition of this book as follows:
Rocklin, Joanne.
Fleabrain loves Franny / by Joanne Rocklin.
pages cm
Summary: "This middle-grade novel takes place in Pittsburgh in 1952–53. The protagonist is Franny, a young girl of imagination, curiosity, and stubbornness. While recovering from polio, she begins a correspondence with a flea named Fleabrain"—Provided by publisher.
Includes bibliographical references.
ISBN 978-1-4197-1068-1 (hardback)
[1. Poliomyelitis—Fiction. 2. People with disabilities—Fiction. 3. Family life—Pennsylvania—Fiction. 4. Fleas—Fiction. 5. Friendship—Fiction. 6. Jews—United States—Fiction. 7. Pittsburgh (Pa.)—History—20th century—Fiction.] I. Title.
PZ7.R59Fle 2014
[Fic]—dc23
2014006380

ISBN for this edition: 978-1-4197-1676-8

Text copyright © 2014 Joanne Rocklin
Cover and title page illustrations © 2014 Kelly Murphy
Book design by Kate Fitch

Printed and bound in USA
10 9 8 7 6 5 4 3 2 1

Amulet Books are available at special discounts when purchased in quantity for premiums and promotions as well as fundraising or educational use. Special editions can also be created to specification. For details, contact specialsales@abramsbooks.com or the address below.

ABRAMS
THE ART OF BOOKS SINCE 1949
115 West 18th Street
New York, NY 10011
www.abramsbooks.com

CONTENTS

III WINTER 1952–53: ADVENTURES

IV SPRING 1953: HOPE

I
SUMMER 1952: QUESTIONS

What Franny Knew

One thing Franny knew. Angels did not exist in real life.

But there they were, floating all around her. Some leaned close, almost touching Franny's nose. Others waved at her from an impossible distance, whizzing about a cathedral ceiling. Their long white robes rustled. Their tiaras sparkled. They hummed and smiled and moved their lips without saying anything, or sometimes they murmured words Franny didn't understand, such as "pachay" and "fee-lee-ah."

Then, one day—

"WOOF!"

—one of the angels barked, sounding remarkably like Franny's dog, Alf.

And Franny awoke from her feverish dreams. She'd only imagined Alf. Pets weren't allowed to visit patients at Children's Hospital, and that's where Franny was, wearing a plastic wristband with FRANCINE

KATZENBACK printed on it. She'd imagined those angels, too, who were actually nurses in white uniforms and peaked caps.

Franny's parents had also been angels in the dreams. They'd stood in the doorway of her hospital room, wearing white masks and worried looks. They couldn't come near her bed because Franny was infectious.

She had polio, everyone told her.

Franny already knew about polio because of her wide and fast reading habits, wider and faster than those of most ten-year-olds. She knew that *polio* was short for *poliomyelitis*. She knew that even though "po-lee-oh" sounded jolly, like "roly-poly," it wasn't.

Franny knew that polio was a disease from a tiny, invisible virus that entered your mouth, stowed away in your intestines, then sometimes burrowed into the nervous system, chomping on nerves so that your limbs became paralyzed. And she knew that the poliovirus could attack your lungs so they couldn't work on their own. When that happened, you needed to lie inside a big, wheezy, green iron tube called an iron lung. The iron lung squeezed your lungs to help you breathe.

But even if Franny hadn't been a wide reader and a fast reader, even if she read only superhero comics like her friend Walter Walter, she'd still know about polio. In her Pittsburgh neighborhood of Squirrel Hill, that summer of 1952, the poliovirus had been practically the only topic of conversation. Polio spread faster during the hot summers. That's what their neighbor Professor Doctor Gutman had told her parents. He was a university professor as well as a researcher, with a long string of letters after his name on the business card he gave Franny's parents. He worked in a lab with the famous polio researcher Dr. Jonas Salk. Everyone knew that Salk and his family also lived in Squirrel Hill, but no one was exactly sure where.

With all that wonderful brainpower in her neighborhood, Franny had felt safe, as if superheroes were ready to protect her from terrible things. How babyish she'd been! Now she knew that nobody, nobody, nobody, not even the brainiest people in the world, knew how to prevent and cure polio. Or why some people got it and the rest didn't.

Lying in her big iron lung, she had a lot of time to think.

Did she get polio by watching *The Story of Robin Hood and His Merrie Men* three whole times at the Manor Theater? Franny and her friends loved that movie. They'd even taken to spelling "merry" the old-fashioned way and threatening to give each other "drubbings" as they swashbuckled around Frick Park. Many people said the evil virus often lurked in crowded movie theaters, but none of the kids believed that.

Or maybe she got it from eating that cherry Popsicle at Sol's Ye Olde Candy Shoppe. Popsicles were absolutely forbidden by all parents because there was a possibility they could be made from contaminated water. So how come other kids in her neighborhood didn't get polio? Teresa Goodly ate more Popsicles than anyone, but she always confessed about it to the priest at her grandmother's church. Maybe that had helped. Jewish kids like Franny didn't go to confession, although Franny was sure it could have been arranged.

The evil virus lurked in pools and lakes, people said, so hardly anyone went swimming anymore, even when the air felt like a hot, wet towel. Franny hadn't swum once that summer.

Walter Walter had said the virus would never get him, because he had a strong constitution. Of course, when your parents give you a first name the same as your last name, and everyone calls you Walter Walter because it's funny, and you feel you have no choice but to go along with the joke, well, that makes you as tough as a tiger, as tough as nails, as tough as raw meat. Double-dose courage and pizzazz. That's what Walter Walter liked to tell everyone.

So how come her own constitution was so weak?

By the time autumn arrived, none of Franny's summer questions had been answered. When she turned her head toward the hospital window, she could see the leaves falling from a scrawny elm tree, disappearing like all the days she'd missed as she lay in her iron lung. An entire Pittsburgh Pirates baseball season, come and gone. Poof! The Pirates had stunk—the worst team of the bunch, people told her. Cellar dwellers! But now she knew that worse things could happen.

Other kids lay in other iron lungs, just their heads sticking out, all together in one big room with Franny, as if they were in a bunch of lifeboats bobbing about in the same rolling ocean. Sometimes the children talked to one another, but most of the time they didn't.

There was a lot of time to think.

There was also a lot of time to cry.

The only good part of Franny's day was when the tutors came, a group of nuns who brought them schoolbooks and storybooks. Franny's tutor was Sister Ed, short for Sister Mary Edberga.

Sister Ed was the first nun Franny had ever known personally. Franny loved her. She was positive Sister Ed was an angel in disguise, even though she smelled a bit like onions, had bushy eyebrows that wriggled like mustaches, and wore a long, dark robe. Franny was sure there were angel wings squashed underneath Sister Ed's habit.

Sister Ed read books out loud like nobody's business. Franny had always imagined that nuns spoke with European accents, like the actress Ingrid Bergman in the movie *The Bells of St. Mary's*. But Sister Ed talked like everyone else in Pittsburgh, except when she was acting out all the parts in the books, using funny voices.

One day Sister Ed arrived, hugging a brand-new book to her chest. "This book is hot off the presses. Just published! You're going to love it! As soon as I read it, I knew it was written for an imaginative kid like you."

The book was about a girl named Fern, who lived on a farm. Fern had a little scared pig named Wilbur. Wilbur's best friend was a kindly spider named Charlotte, who protected him and wrote compliments inside her web. For example, *SOME PIG*. Everyone on the farm was just knocked out and flabbergasted by Charlotte's talents! Other amazing things happened at that farm, with Charlotte's help.

Miracles.

"Read it again," Franny said when Sister Ed came to the last page.

And Sister Ed did, as many times as Franny wanted, or a favorite chapter or two on request. When Franny wanted to sleep, she asked Sister Ed to sing the lullaby Charlotte sang to Wilbur. Sister Ed sang different tunes at different times, but the words were always the same.

Sleep, sleep, my love, my only,
Deep, deep, in the dung and the dark . . .

Sometimes Franny pretended she was Fern, living on a country farm with all those barnyard animals, instead of in busy, car-honking Pittsburgh. But she marveled that they both lived in Pennsylvania, she and Fern. Sometimes she pretended she was Wilbur the pig, who had a miraculous friend like Charlotte.

Soon the doctors decided it was time Franny practiced breathing on her own. But outside of the iron lung, like a fish thrashing on a riverbank, Franny couldn't get her lungs to work. She was suffocating! She decided it wasn't a bad thing to live forever inside an iron tube, waiting for Sister Ed to read stories to her.

One afternoon Sister Ed said, in her big jolly voice, "Hey, kid, take a look at this!"

She was pointing to a spiderweb on the wall. Who did Sister Ed think she was kidding? Even from the iron lung Franny could see that it was just a pencil drawing of a spiderweb. Inside the web, in tall, black script, somebody (Franny's guess: Sister Ed) had written

SOME GIRL

"Imagine this spiderweb is the real deal," said Sister Ed. "Please, Franny. Imagine."

Each day the nurses and orderlies pulled Franny from the iron lung so she could practice her breathing, and each day Sister Ed pointed to that web.

"Imagine! Imagine!" boomed Sister Ed.

And each day Franny could breathe a few more minutes on her own. Sister Ed said she wasn't surprised. She said she had faith all along that Franny could do it. So Franny tried to have faith, too, and after a while she didn't need the iron lung at all. The doctors said it was time for Franny to go home to her family. Franny had been hoping to go home all along, deep down in her heart of hearts.

"Charlotte helped me like she helped Wilbur," Franny said. She was going home in a wheelchair because she couldn't walk yet. But she was out of that green iron lung, and she could breathe.

Sister Ed wriggled her eyebrows and kissed her good-bye. "The story isn't over," she said. Then she gave Franny the book, *Charlotte's Web*, for keeps.

Franny prayed that one day she would witness a miracle as real and fine as that spider, Charlotte.

And she did.

II
AUTUMN 1952: CORRESPONDENCE

The Note from Nowhere

Franny had been home from the hospital ten days before she found the note.

It was on her bed, which was strewn with schoolbooks, library books, Get Well cards, and that week's assignments delivered on Monday afternoons by her teacher, Mrs. Nelson. The note was half-hidden by a ball of dust and dog hair, underneath one of her books. In the Katzenback household, if there were any dust balls to be found, they were usually under beds, not on top of them. So, first Franny was surprised to notice the dust ball, and then she was even more surprised to see the scrap of paper folded inside it. The ink was a rich chocolatey-brown, the unfamiliar handwriting tiny yet elegant. Some letters leaned forward as if in a hurry to have their say; others stretched their long legs athletically. Every now and then the words themselves leaped about the page.

Franny held up the note to the window, squinting to read it.

Greetings, Franny,

Bonjour! Now that you've found my note, you can stop
seeking messages
in spiderwebs. Only one bug we know
composed that way, and she's

unique.

And need I remind you, also
fictional?
Besides which, her output was meager
and pedestrian and sentimental,
although
that's probably beside the
point . . .
    I, Fleabrain, have much more to offer!
    I offer you an invitation
                to connect.
    So,
répondez s'il vous plaît, which I know I don't have to
translate for
    you, Franny.
        Cordially,
        Fleabrain

Franny flopped down onto her pillow. Resting at the foot of her
bed, Alf opened an eye, saw that Franny was OK, then went back to
sleep.

How humiliating! Franny thought. Her private wishes revealed!

Yes, she'd been searching for spiderwebs lately, because of that book. That wonderful, wonderful book! Unfortunately, to her knowledge, there weren't any webs to be found inside the house, especially because an invalid lived there now and everything had to be kept extra scrupulously clean. And there were absolutely no bugs, either. Fly spray and ant hotels and Alf's flea powder took care of that.

Still, Min had guessed! Of course it was Min who had cleverly disguised her handwriting and put the dust ball and its note on her bed. Just to torment her.

Min must have guessed that time she'd been pushing Franny in her wheelchair down the block, when Franny had leaned way, way to the side to get a good look at the spiderweb draped on Mrs. Kramer's shrub rose. Franny had been absolutely positive she'd seen a Capital *T* for *Terrific* in that web.

"Franny!" Min had hollered. "What the huckleberry are you doing?"

Now Franny stared at the ceiling, thinking how much she hated her older sister. She really, really did. Sometimes it felt so good to hate her, like picking at a knee scab. When she used to have knee scabs.

"*Huckleberry*, my foot, Min," said Franny. "You think you're so great, you can't even say *HECK*!"

And it felt so good to say *HECK*.

Alf sat up. "Hey, it's OK, Alf," said Franny. The dog gave his neck a good scratch with his hind leg, then lay down again.

Heck wasn't nearly as bad as that horrible word in the note.

PEDESTRIAN. How mean of Min to bring up a certain topic in a sneaky way, while pretending to talk about spiders!

Pedestrian.

A person who walks.

I'll show her, thought Franny. She popped the tiny note into her mouth, chewed hard, then swallowed. *I never even saw your note, Min! So there.*

The note left an odd but familiar taste in her mouth.

What Fleabrain Knew

leabrain was composing a small poem in his microscopic head. He was usually inspired to do so when he thought about the catastrophe. Poetry helped soothe his terrible loneliness, not to mention the terrible guilt.

A tragedy of epic size.
Oh, their cries!
Each and every one, a ghastly demise.
Seventy-two thousand and ten
Women, children, men,
The eggs, as well (but one),
Pearly and translucent
And, oh! So innocent!

He supposed it was a miracle he alone had survived the deadly flea powder. Not to mention the miracle of his lofty intelligence quotient! There was so much to know! So many wonderful books to read in this one house alone.

But, bug it! He didn't feel at all miraculous. He simply felt alone. Small, small, small, and so alone! Mutated and transmogrified from a pearly egg to a freak.

Great knowledge was useless unless shared with like minds.

Also, he wanted his mama.

And his dad, too.

He comforted himself, remembering the story of his parents' romantic meeting.

On that fateful day, Min Katzenback and the dog Alf had been strolling by the horse stables in Frick Park. In an instant, Min fell in love with Milt, the stable boy. And, in an instant, Fleabrain's dad had fallen in love with Fleabrain's mom. His dad had been a lone flea among the ticks on a horse named Lightning. Fleabrain's dad noticed Fleabrain's lovely mom clinging to the dog Alf's tail. His dad leaped from the horse to join her on Alf, smitten for the remainder of his life. The rest was history.

A short life and a short history, as it happened, because of the flea powder.

Fleabrain would have so enjoyed getting to know his twenty immediate siblings in his particular batch of eggs, not to mention his countless other siblings and cousins.

He would have loved them all, IQ or no IQ. He was no snob.

Then again, could his family have loved him back, without a smidgen of IQ? Ah, love! Intelligence brings its own rewards. But what good was so much love in his heart—OK, his primitive pumping mechanism—with no one with whom to share it?

And, oh, how he longed for the simple pleasure of a sip of blood without the guilt! The guilt!

Knowledge brought guilt.

Bug it! He knew way too much.

Reading and writing poetry helped. He was proud of his own rhymes. *Cries* and *demise*, especially.

He hoped she'd write back.

Franny's Answer

A tap on her bedroom door.

"Did you call me?"

It was Min.

"No," said Franny.

Min poked her head into the room. "I thought you just did."

"Well, I didn't," said Franny. And then she couldn't hold back. "I know you wrote it!"

Min frowned. She came into the room and leaned down to kiss Alf's ear. "Wrote what?"

"That dumb note!"

"What the huckleberry are you talking about?"

Franny stared hard at her sister, answering with a silence she hoped seemed stony and forbidding. But, again, she couldn't keep it in.

"Here's a small hint for you: *Fleabrain!*"

Min blinked. Her cheeks turned red, and she pulled on her short brown ponytail. But then she smiled her kind, sympathetic, and nurse-y smile, the too-old-for-a-fifteen-year-old smile she'd been smiling at Franny ever since Franny got sick.

"Are you having a hard time today?" Min asked. "I'm really sorry."

Now, before she got sick, Franny had been the actress, the one with the imagination, the dreamer, the spinner of tales. Franny, for instance, was the one who had perfected that imitation of Queen Elizabeth, waving her hand from side to side in a regal way. She was the one who could sound like Jiminy Cricket, or their mom on the telephone with their aunt Pauline, or Alf describing his life as a dog.

But here was Min, doing a pretty good imitation of someone who had never disguised her handwriting and left a dumb note on some- one else's bed.

"You know. The note!" Franny said.

Min wrinkled her brow. "What note?" she asked.

All of a sudden Franny knew that she *didn't* know. Min wouldn't have left that note on her bed, because she would never have teased her like that, using the word *pedestrian*. Min was kind. And that's why, strange to say, Franny sort of hated her. Also, she wouldn't even have known how to spell *pedestrian*. And she had terrible handwriting, no matter how hard she practiced her penmanship.

"Maybe you have a fever," said Min, placing her cool hand on Franny's forehead.

"I probably do," said Franny. That would explain everything.

"I'll go get help," said Min with a frightened look, and she raced out of the room.

Fever was what had started everything in the first place, that burning-up fever trying so hard to fight off the poliovirus, which it wasn't able to do. And then, when the fever had run its course, Franny hadn't been a *pedestrian* anymore.

It was Sunday, and her parents' store, Katzenback's Footwear, was closed. Now they stood nervously by Franny's bed, along with Nurse Olivegarten, who'd just arrived. Alf joyously sniffed everybody. Alf was always excited to have visitors, hoping for a party with crumbly cookies from the Waldorf Bakery. There hadn't been many celebrations in the Katzenback home lately.

"No fever," Franny's mom said, laying her hand on Franny's forehead, using her Thermometer Powers.

Nurse Olivegarten frowned, obviously preferring medical science over Thermometer Powers.

The first time they'd met, Franny had thought Nurse Olivegarten had a face like a movie star. She was a real "looker," her parents said, with her rosy cheeks and flashing white teeth and her big eyes as green as—yes—green olives. She sounded like an actress, too, because of her la-di-da Canadian accent. And you could tell she had a figure like a movie star's hiding under her nurse's uniform.

But it was hard to remember that Nurse Olivegarten was pretty. Compared to her, Sister Ed was the movie star, despite Sister Ed's eyebrows. That's because Nurse Olivegarten always looked as if she were sucking on—yes—the pit of an olive. And even though Nurse Olivegarten "came highly recommended," Franny knew she had a meanness inside of her. That meanness seeped out and made her ugly, just like the humans transmogrified into aliens in those science-fiction movies she and Walter Walter enjoyed.

Nurse Olivegarten had pinched her once when nobody was looking. Maybe twice. Franny never told anybody, because Nurse Olivegarten came so highly recommended. She had been trained in a special, surefire method, using hot packs and stretching, developed by a famous Australian nurse named Sister Kenny. Nurse Olivegarten promised she was going to make Franny walk again, by hook or by crook. And as soon as Franny's pediatrician certified she was no longer contagious and had some mobility, Franny could return to Creswell School, Principal Woolcott had told her parents.

Now Nurse Olivegarten pulled a real thermometer from her medical bag, and Franny opened her mouth for it.

No one spoke during the long minutes before her mother leaned over Nurse Olivegarten's shoulder to read the results.

"No fever!" her mother pronounced again, with a relieved and triumphant smile.

And then it was time for Franny's morning treatment, as it always was at 9:00 A.M. and again at 4:00 P.M. She put her arms around her father's neck. He lifted her up and carried her into the kitchen, where he laid her down on the towel-draped kitchen table.

Her father went to stir something on the stove. Franny could smell the oil and herbs warming in their secret, magic, massage concoction. Nurse Olivegarten didn't approve of that concoction. She said it was "hocus-pocus." But it was the best part of Franny's treatment. The worst part came first.

First Nurse Olivegarten used burning-hot, wet, woolen packs to loosen Franny's leg muscles. Then she supervised as Franny's parents took turns stretching and bending Franny's legs. "Stretch long and stretch hard," Nurse Olivegarten said, bending over Franny's body, her eyes narrowing critically.

"That hurts!" cried Franny.

"I can't stand to see her in pain," her mother said.

"Pain never hurt anybody," said Nurse Olivegarten. Under normal circumstances, that would have made Franny laugh. But now she clenched her teeth and her fists and counted the cracks in the ceiling.

"You *do* want your girl to walk again, eh?" asked Nurse Olivegarten.

Her mother nodded, lips trembling.

Often, so she herself wouldn't cry as she lay there, Franny tried to get angry instead. She would make up a list of all the things she hated in the world, in alphabetical order. When she reached *Z*, she would begin all over again. There were always things she'd left out the time before.

Hills. **I**llness. **J**unk drawers.

Knuckle-cracking. **L**ima beans. **L**amp fixture on the ceiling, shining into her eyes. **M**ice in the walls.

Notes from **N**owhere.

People named **O**live. Real **o**lives, too, from now on.

Pedestrians.

Franny suddenly remembered something. *Pedestrian* had more than one meaning!

"Some note," she said, to no one in particular.

"Which note, darling?" asked her mother. Franny received many Get Well cards in the mail. Walter Walter slipped one under their front door almost every week.

"Nothing, nothing," Franny said.

Of course her mom or dad hadn't written the note, either. Her parents read many books and kept practically every book they'd ever owned, even their high school and college textbooks, in the lofty bookcase in the front hall. But Franny had never witnessed them reading any juvenile fiction, not since Franny herself became a wide and fast reader and no longer needed her parents to read to her. Franny had highly recommended *Charlotte's Web*, but her mother had a fear of bugs, especially spiders. Even saintly, fictional ones. She used much more bug spray than was necessary, in Franny's opinion.

Nurse Olivegarten had just arrived, so it couldn't have been her.

Franny realized she didn't actually hate the Note from Nowhere. She felt curious about its oddness, like when she'd tasted an oyster for the first time, immediately wanting another one. She could still taste the note in her mouth, although it didn't taste at all oysterish.

After her leg massage with her dad's secret, magic potion (and even if it wasn't really magic, the massage felt lovely), her father carried her to her bedroom, leaving her alone to rest.

As soon as he left the room, Franny leaned over and reached for her journal and a pencil. She licked the pencil so her writing would be nice and dark, and wrote

Charlotte is wonderful and interesting and unique! Not pedestrian at all!!!

"Répondez s'il vous plaît?" you ask.

OK, I will.

Who the HECK are you?

Waiting

Franny was getting used to waiting. She'd never waited so much in her whole entire life.

She waited for the sun to brighten her drawn curtains. The darkness frightened her.

She waited for her parents to carry her to the bathroom and help her dress and then bring breakfast in bed. Breakfast in bed used to be a special treat. Not anymore.

She waited, her heart thumping, for Nurse Olivegarten to arrive. She waited, with clenched fists, for Nurse Olivegarten to leave.

Blisters. **C**hills. **D**irt.

Eggs, rotten.

Fish, spoiled.

Garlic, lately. Franny knew that the kids in her neighborhood wore sacks of garlic around their necks so they wouldn't get polio.

She waited for the angels to come again, and then she waited to wake up and discover it was all a bad dream and there was no such thing as polio. She could walk and run like everyone else, and the only wheels she needed were on her bike. Maybe she'd wake up to find that polio was a game everyone played, like Capture the Flag. Except it was Capture the Flag Pole-Ee-Oh. Or something.

And, of course, Franny waited for another Note from Nowhere. It had been over two weeks.

When Franny read a book, the waiting stopped. Pittsburgh time slipped away when she was reading, and only the hours of other worlds were true. Being a wide and fast reader, she could finish a book in two days. One, if the book was short.

Franny was rereading *Charlotte's Web*, even though she practically knew the whole book by heart and could answer any and all trivia questions about it. Not that anything concerning that book was trivial! *Charlotte's Web* was about everything important—for example, birth and death and love and the glory of everything.

But being a *Charlotte's Web* expert was not a useful talent, as talents go, unless she went on a radio quiz show.

"WHAT WAS THE NAME OF THE HUMAN PROTAGONIST IN THE STORY?"

"Easy-peasy. Her name begins with the letter *F*, like mine. Fern!"

"WHERE WAS FERN'S FATHER GOING WITH THAT AX?"

"To the hog house to kill the smallest pig."

"PIG'S NAME?"

"Wilbur!"

"WHICH ONE WAS THE RODENT, CHARLOTTE OR TEMPLETON?"

"Templeton!"

"WHO WAS WILBUR'S TRUEST FRIEND?"

"Charlotte!"

"WHAT IS THE CAPITAL OF PENNSYLVANIA?"

"Harrisburg!"

"ALL CORRECT FOR ONE THOUSAND DOLLARS AND THE OPPORTUNITY TO BE A CONTESTANT ON *QUIZ KIDS* AGAIN!"

If she went on a radio quiz show, nobody would see that she wasn't a pedestrian. When President Roosevelt had been president, ordinary, regular citizens hadn't known he had polio and had to get around in a wheelchair. Ordinary, regular citizens only saw him in newsreels at the movies, looking perfectly fine behind a desk, or they heard his comforting presidential voice crackling through the radio.

But she wasn't a winner on a quiz show, or Fern on that happy farm in Harrisburg, Pennsylvania. She was Franny in Squirrel Hill, Pennsylvania, stuck in a wheelchair in her bedroom.

True, she did like her bedroom. She liked its pale yellow walls, the color of custard. She liked her bright new yellow afghan on the bed. The dancing ballerina on the face of her alarm clock. Her multicolored braided rug on the floor. Her matching oak headboard, bookcase, desk, and night table—seven scratches on the desktop, two water stains on the night table. All her new books in the bookcase (they'd burned her old ones because of possible polio germs). The funny-looking dracaena plant by the window, a Get Well gift from the staff at Katzenback's Footwear. Whenever Franny looked at it, the plant seemed to wriggle its messy hairdo of leaves, as if to say, "Cheer up! Cheer up!"

She liked her bedroom; she really did. But she knew every inch of it much too well.

Franny gave a deep sigh. She pushed herself to her night table to get her baseball. She kept it in full view, to remind herself that even though her legs were bad, her right arm was still pretty good. She rolled her chair to the window, removed its screen, then held the ball in the cleft between the pointing and middle finger of her right hand. Then she aimed at the stretch of Shady Avenue where the hilly part of the street leveled out.

WHOOSH!

Franny's Whiz Ball.

The ball flew out the window, bounced across the street, hit the curb, then rolled under a parked car.

"Strike one!" she said.

Alf stirred at the foot of her wheelchair.

"WOOF!" he barked, eyes pleading.

"I know, I know," Franny said. "You want to go out. You need a pedestrian for that, old pal, and that's not me. Hey, don't worry. You may not be Wilbur the pig, but I still love you."

Franny reached over to tickle his nose. Alf whined, as if he had something very important to tell her.

Min had heard Alf's whine and came into the room. "Let's all go for a walk. Me, you, and Alf," she said.

"No. You take Alf," Franny said. "And please get my ball from under Mr. Avery's Dodge while you're out."

Franny didn't know what she hated most—all those eyes staring at her in her wheelchair or all those eyes pretending not to see her at all. And it was such a humiliating, exhausting ordeal! First her chair had to be carted down the front stairs. Then she had to be carried like a baby by her mother or father and Saint Min, to be plunked into her wheelchair in front of the whole world. Pittsburgh itself was a city of hills and stairways, which Franny had never really thought about Before. Now each stair, each knoll, each bumpy sidewalk was a taunt, reminding her of all that had changed.

"Please, Franny," Min said. "It's a nice day. We won't have too many more before winter."

It was more than a nice day. It was a Saturday morning that felt like the opening scene in a movie, an orchestra playing in the background, the sun blazing, the sky bright blue, sparrows chirping, autumn-bright leaves—all that, except it was real life. Even from the window, Franny could tell.

"Oh, fine," Franny said.

And even in her wheelchair, being helped along by Saint Min (after Min had retrieved the baseball), with Alf running along beside them, for a few minutes Franny was glad she didn't live on Fern's farm. She was glad to be outside on such a lovely day in good old Squirrel Hill. Just like Before. For a few minutes, Franny forgot she wasn't a pedestrian.

But only for a few minutes. She could hear Min huffing and puffing as she pushed Franny's wheelchair toward Frick Park. Of course. Min wanted an excuse to bat her eyelashes at Milt, who was at the stables in the park every Saturday morning. Franny didn't really mind, because she liked Milt. And she adored Lightning, the aging former racehorse in the second stall.

"Hi, you two," Milt said when he saw them rounding the stony path. "Great wheels, Franny! Have you popped any wheelies yet?"

It felt so good when Milt teased her like a regular girl instead of an invalid to be treated like a delicate fern from a nursery.

"Not yet," said Franny. "But maybe soon, *langer loksh*."

Milt was tall and skinny. Franny's great-grandfather Zadie Ben called him a *langer loksh*, which meant a "long noodle" in Yiddish, and so everyone else in the family called him that, too.

Min and Milt made a handsome pair. Unlike Franny, who was short, Min was tall. Franny and Min looked very much alike, with their wavy brown hair, pale skin, and eyeglasses, but Min looked like the stretched-out gum-band version. At the moment, Milt and Min only had eyes for one another, although they weren't really batting them, Franny noticed. She decided to wheel herself over to the second stall to visit Lightning while Milt and Min sat under a tree.

"Hey, old Secret Keeper. Long time no see," Franny said, reaching way up to pat the handsome bay's nose. "Too bad neither of us can sprint anymore."

Lightning nuzzled Franny's neck, then looked right into her eyes. His own kind, dark eyes encouraged secrets, and Franny suspected that many kids had whispered private things into Lightning's warm, odorous ears, just as she did. They knew he'd keep their secrets safe, always and forever.

Voices drifted over a hill, and Franny turned to see the Pack strolling toward her. The Pack consisted of Walter Walter; his brother, Seymour; Teresa Goodly; her little sister, Rose; the new girl, Quiet Katy Green; and the Solomon siblings, A (Albert), B (Bobby), and C (Carol). Franny herself used to be a bona fide member of the Pack, Before. All of them smiled at Franny as they approached the stables, but then, as if responding to a high-pitched signal only they could hear, they hurried past her toward Beechwood Boulevard.

"Whoa!" shouted Franny. "Where are you going? Fire? Parade? Circus in town?"

Or something.

Franny knew where they were going. Away from her, that's where.

"Hey, guess what?" she yelled. "I'm not contagious anymore!"

Accompanied by a pungent whiff of garlic, Walter Walter turned and walked toward her, but not too close. He was carrying his bat.

"Thanks for the six Get Well cards," said Franny.

"Seven," said Walter Walter with a small smile.

"Right. Seven. Hey, you still wearing that stupid thing around your neck?" Franny asked.

Walter Walter shrugged, glancing down at the little bag attached to a string.

"I guess," he said. "They say it works."

"Who's 'they'?"

Walter Walter shrugged again. "People. I don't know."

"Walter Walter, you tell me how a bulb of garlic can fight the poliovirus! Go on. Bet you can't!"

"Virus hates the smell?"

"That's stupid, and you know it."

"Well, all the kids are wearing garlic. Nobody's caught polio yet."

"So you're saying if I'd worn a stinky bag of garlic around my neck, then I wouldn't have gotten it?"

"Don't know," said Walter Walter. He swung his bat at an imaginary pitch, then stopped swinging. "Why'd you get polio, anyway? Nobody else did. I heard they burned all your old books and toys and stuff because everything you touched was contagious."

"That was then. But they say I'm not contagious now. I'll be going back to school once I'm more 'independently mobile.' And nobody knows why I got it."

"Who's 'they'?"

His pleading eyes stared right into hers. Franny could tell Walter Walter wasn't being a smart aleck. He really wanted to know.

"Smart people. Doctors," Franny said. "People who know how viruses operate. My pediatrician told us I'm definitely not contagious at this point. And neither is my mother or my father or Min. Viruses are like villains who ride into town, shoot like crazy, then gallop away, leaving death and destruction in their wake."

Walter Walter was silent, leaning on his bat.

Franny held up her baseball. "Feel like hitting a few? I can still throw."

"No time," said Walter Walter, looking guilty. "We're getting a game together at the school yard in a few minutes." He brightened suddenly, reaching into his pocket. "Hey, I've been meaning to give you these buckeyes, since you couldn't gather them yourself this year. They should be as hard as rocks by spring. You'll be OK by spring, right?"

"Of course," Franny said.

In the autumn, round buckeye nuts, as big as half-dollars, fell from the horse chestnut trees growing in Homewood Cemetery. After the nuts had dried over the winter, they were cherished and traded by the Pack as if they were expensive marbles, or they were tied to spare shoelaces like mini-catapults for the Pack's buckeye-slinging contests.

"Here you go," Walter Walter said. He dropped four round buckeyes into Franny's outstretched palm.

"Thank you," said Franny. "I didn't think I'd have any this year." Franny noticed that Walter Walter had been very, very careful not to touch her. She put the buckeyes into her pocket. "Hey, Mr. Double-Dose Pizzazz Walter Walter," she said suddenly, leaning forward as if she had a secret to share. "Want to be a real superhero?"

"What?"

"You heard me. It's easy-peasy." Franny held out her hand. "Here. Shake."

Walter Walter looked at Franny's outstretched hand. He didn't move.

"No viruses on it anywhere. I promise. Come on, shake!" Franny wriggled her fingers. "And tell the others to come by, too."

Franny waited.

The seconds ticked by.

One. Two. Three.

Four. Five. Six.

A second for every year they'd been friends.

Walter Walter gently tapped Franny's outstretched fingers with the tip of his bat.

"Hey!" cried Franny.

They stared at one another, eyes wide. Franny could tell Walter Walter was as surprised as she was at what he'd just done.

"I'm really sorry, Franny. I hope you get better. Maybe I'll come visit soon, OK? My parents..." Then Walter Walter turned and raced away to catch up with the others.

Franny shouted after him. "You'll never be a real superhero! You're a yellow-bellied, lily-livered milksop!"

That night Franny picked at her chicken leg during supper, brushed Alf while they both lay in her bed, threw a book across the room (*Little Women*, not *Charlotte's Web*), counted all the reasons she hated Walter Walter and other kids she knew, cried until she was too tired to cry anymore, and was just about to turn off her lamp, when she noticed the tiny chocolatey-brown writing in her journal.

Greetings, Franny!
Bonjour! At last
we connect!
"Who the HECK" am I?
Ich bin Fleabrain.
Je m'appelle Fleabrain.
Yo soy Fleabrain.
我是 Fleabrain.
I am a proud representative of Ctenocephalides canis,
flea of the dog.

I am thrilled to share
my thoughts about books and culture

with

you.

I am enjoying the plethora of books in the Katzenback bookshelves

and have completed the works of that Englishman William Shakespeare (April 23, 1564–April 23, 1616).

I have also recently read Die Verwandlung by Franz Kafka (July 3, 1883–June 3, 1924), who was from Prague but wrote in German.

Have you read it? Terribly overrated. It is a story about a man who turns into a bug overnight. I was rather offended by its silly, buggist plot. Can't wait to discuss!

Not to brag, but I complete

one great work by a preeminent thinker almost every day,

often two great works, depending upon how long they take to digest.

Happily,

FB

P.S. Dare I add a bashful little postscript? Well, here it is: Would you be so kind as to meet me at the tip of Alf's tail, tomorrow after your evening treatment, around 5:30 p.m.?

Yours,

Fleabrain

Other Things Fleabrain Knew

Fleabrain knew—he knew with all his heart, with every cell of his minute, ugly body—that he and she were Kindred Spirits. Spirits in Kind.

("Ugly" was a relative term. His mama, whom he resembled, would have found him handsome and dapper. But if he were human-size, he'd be a monster.)

In fact . . .

. . . he knew he loved Franny.

And, as the English poet Elizabeth Barrett Browning, born March 6, 1806, died June 29, 1861, once wrote in her moving poem "How do I love thee? Let me count the ways . . . ," his own microscopic brain enjoyed counting the ways that he, Fleabrain, loved Franny:

1. Both were attached to the same dog.
2. Both of their names began with *F.*
3. Both felt small. Emphasis: *felt.*
4. Both felt invisible. Emphasis: *felt.*

5. Both were lonely.

6. Both had feelings about Charlotte. True, not the same feelings. (Yes, he was bitterly jealous of Franny's adoration of that storybook arachnid. Certainly not proud of that, he had to admit.)

7. But, oh, how they both loved books! He himself was more than halfway through the texts of that lofty hallway bookcase, having absorbed treatises on geometry, philosophy, first aid, calculus, European history, and more. He was now gobbling up the foreign-language shelves. Spanish conversation. The French essayists. The German poets and philosophers. How clever of humans to communicate in a variety of languages. Nonhumans had only the Language of Instinct. Reliable, yet often limiting.

Bug it! He, Fleabrain, with his ever-reliable instincts, his marvelous, brilliant brain, and his loving heart, knew that he and Franny could be the very, very best of friends. She didn't really need any others.

He could hardly wait to meet in person (so to speak)!

Believing

Franny believed.

She believed the Earth was wondrous, as was its plant-making Sun and tide-making Moon. She also believed there was life on other spinning planets, somewhere in the dark mystery of space. An infinity of wondrousness.

Teresa believed in God, who looked like a combination of Santa and her kindly great-uncle Donald, she said. But sometimes Teresa imagined God resembling Uncle Donald's wife, Marie, also kindly, who made heavenly snickerdoodles.

Min believed God looked like Rabbi Hailperin, in a stylish suit and tie under his prayer shawl. Of course, she was sophisticated enough to know otherwise, she said, but that's what she imagined during services.

Quiet Katy, the new girl, hardly ever said anything about anything. But one day she blurted out that she didn't really know for sure what she thought about God. Maybe God was just a good feeling and didn't look like anyone at all.

Walter Walter believed in aliens. Most of them had gigantic eyes and blinking spokes for ears. They always commanded magnificent flying machines. He was positive they were out there, but Franny wasn't so sure.

In *Charlotte's Web*, Fern had fervently believed in Charlotte. In *Peter Pan*, Wendy had believed in Tinker Bell and Never Never Land. True, those kids lived in books, but it had all seemed so real, Franny had believed, too! And wasn't *that* kind of wondrous?

There were so many possibilities to believe in.

There were so many things, good and bad, that nobody could prove or understand.

But Franny believed—she *knew*—that there were invisible alien viruses that could turn you into another person one fine morning, a person who could no longer walk. Nothing ever again could surprise her as much as knowing that.

So Franny believed in a tiny flea, mutated and transmogrified into a writer of splendid notes.

Fleabrain.

At 5:30 p.m. the next evening, Franny checked the tip of Alf's tail. Alf lay patiently stretched out on Franny's coverlet, big head on big front paws. There had been no mention of a particular hair at which to meet, tip or otherwise. Franny combed through Alf's entire bushy tail with her fingers. Unfortunately, Alf's tail was darker in color than the rest of him. Something unusual would be difficult to spot. At one point Franny thought she saw a speck flit across one hair, but she couldn't find it again.

That night Franny whispered into the darkness, "Are you there? Will we ever meet? Are you really just a flea?"

At the bottom of the bed, Alf didn't stir, as if he knew Franny's three questions were not for him.

By the Light of the Moon

Fleabrain had hollered. He had leaped. He had shaken his tibiae, frantic to communicate. He'd tried clapping his tarsi, clattering his mouthparts, and frantically raising the short hairs on his back, the latter considered an impertinent gesture among his kind. He had been desperate for Franny's attention and was weak from his exertions.

Fleabrain heard Franny whispering her three lonely questions into the darkness. Replenished after supping on Alf, he was inspired to write a poem in Franny's journal by the light of the moon. How gratifying it felt to translate his angst into a creative endeavor!

Unfortunately, by daybreak he realized his creation was not up to his usual standards. To wit, it was a very bad poem, and it was too late to revise it. It had been written in haste and frustration, though not without love.

Nevertheless, in his heart he knew Franny would understand and perhaps even appreciate his literary effort.

Franny—
I wail
To no avail
From a hair on Alf's tail.
Yes! Three times yes!
But to hear me, you fail.

P.S. My dear Franny, the above is a work in progress. There is, one might say, "avail" available. So, yes, three times yes, to your questions.
We will find a way.
Yours,
FB

P.S. Hopefully, you will eventually think of me as more than "just a flea"
and
as a cherished friend.

The Bookcase

T
he day after receiving the very bad poem, which (as Fleabrain had hoped) she enjoyed for its clarity and honesty, Franny wheeled herself to the entry-hall bookcase, hoping to spot Fleabrain among its "plethora" of books.

Like Fleabrain, Franny loved the books in that bookcase. Some of the books used to belong to Franny's deceased grandparents and great-grandparents; others her parents had bought cheaply in used bookstores. They had their own odor, ancient and mysteriously adult, smelling of woolen blankets and socks and soup and exhaust fumes and classrooms. That's because the books were read in all sorts of places before they ended up in the bookcase. Many, many people had loved them.

Franny's parents had read most of the books in high school and college. They often said they hardly remembered what was in them, even though all of their schooling had been an "enlightening experience." Mr. and Mrs. Katzenback preferred reading about current events in newspapers. But her mother respectfully dusted off the tops of the books once a year, and both of her parents said the tall, lofty bookcase made for a handsome entryway.

Franny didn't really understand how her parents' schooling could have been enlightening if they'd forgotten almost all of it. She herself resolved to remember every bit of the higher learning of her life. The lower learning, too. Why else bother learning? Her parents didn't want her nosing around "adult" books, which, of course, made the books more enticing, even though she hardly understood most of them.

"Hello, hello," Franny whispered, opening a few books at random. She imagined letters and words and paragraphs dancing in a dusty, happy cloud from the yellowing pages, grateful to be alive again. *Wheeee! We're free-eeeee! Hello, hello to you, too!* She hoped that Fleabrain would emerge from one of the books. But if he did, she didn't see him.

As she didn't know German, Franny had never read *Die Verwandlung*, the book Fleabrain had deemed "buggist" and overrated. But she did know it for its strange and deliciously horrifying book jacket. She decided to build up the courage to face the frightening jacket by first leafing through the French texts from her parents' college days. Many of the books in the bookshelves had underlining and circled phrases and cryptic comments in the margins. But the French texts contained the love notes.

Je t'adore, Muriel.
Je t'adore, Sammy.
Sammy. Mon cher.
Muriel. Mon petit choux.

There were lots more mushy-sounding notes scribbled in the margins of the books. Franny's parents, Muriel and Sammy, had fallen in love during university French class. They'd given their daughters French names, Minot and Francine, to commemorate their love. Franny enjoyed discovering those notes. They made her think of chocolate-covered caramels and lacy valentines. Although sometimes she wished her parents had written on a variety of topics in order to practice their French. Then they could have passed on that fluency to their offspring.

Finally, her hand trembling, Franny reached for the small, thin book with the faded red spine.

DIE VERWANDLUNG. Franz Kafka.

What did *Die Verwandlung* mean, anyway? *Die? Wand? Lung?*

There were penciled exclamation marks scattered in the margins, and someone had scribbled *Kafka has the answers* in a margin. Another person had excitedly responded, *HE DOES! HE DOES!*

The book had been purchased in a used bookstore by Sam Katzenback, but he'd never read it, having dropped German literature and conversation for French literature and conversation after his first day of class, in order to meet the lovely Muriel, he said. Franny wished he'd remained in the class so that he'd be able to translate this strange book for his future daughter. Of course, if he'd remained in the German class and never met Muriel, his future daughter wouldn't have been Franny.

Franny forced herself to carefully examine the Kafka book jacket again.

A giant-size insect lay on its back, waving its scaly tentacles. Its eyes were unseeing mounds in its forehead. Its mouth was a grimacing circle of sharp fangs.

But what made the illustration peculiarly horrifying was that the giant-size insect was lying on a four-poster bed, covered by a blue and white checkered quilt. A man's brown leather slippers, toes touching, were by the bed, waiting for a man's feet to slip into them. Newspapers were scattered on the patterned rug. A jug of water sat on a night table, and a white shirt and brown suspenders were draped over a chair.

Horrifying! Deliciously, shiver-inspiringly horrifying. Almost funny.

And yet.

So, so sad.

Why was the bug lying in bed? Why did the bug own human clothes?

Franny stared intently at the illustration. The more she looked at it, the more fascinating and interesting it became. The bug's fanged mouth opened wide, then snapped shut. Franny blinked. *Open, snap!* As if the bug were trying to answer her questions!

"Oh!" cried Franny, startled. The book dropped from her hands to the floor. Straining forward to reach for it, she toppled to the floor herself.

"For goodness' sake, girl!"

Nurse Olivegarten raced down the hall from the bathroom, where she'd been smoking a cigarette. She probably thought no one knew, but Franny sure did. Franny could smell that cigarette no matter how much lilac perfume and peppermint mouthwash Nurse Olivegarten used.

"I told you to wait by the bathroom door," said Nurse Olivegarten into Franny's ear. She pulled her back into her wheelchair, squeezing Franny's shoulders, hard.

"What was that thump?" asked Franny's mother, emerging from the kitchen, Alf bounding behind her. "Franny, are you hurt?"

"I'm fine." Franny quickly hid *Die Verwandlung* behind her back and then sat on it. Suddenly she realized who could translate it for her. "It's a nice day," she said. "Can't we go out for a walk and meet Dad at the streetcar stop?"

Her father had taken the streetcar downtown to work that day because the family car was in the shop. It was Professor Doctor Gutman's stop, too, and he and her father sometimes strolled home together. Professor Doctor Gutman spoke English with what sounded to Franny like a German accent! On the walk back to Shady Avenue she could casually ask him about *Die Verwandlung* and find out why Kafka had all the answers. Or at least invite him for supper one evening to discuss the book further, after which she could discuss it with Fleabrain.

"A walk! Impossible!" said Nurse Olivegarten, her mouth twisting into a fake smile, as if a joke had been made about Franny's ability to walk. "We've done too much today. My shift is over, and I must start home."

"Franny, it's almost dusk," said her mother.

"We can all go with Nurse Olivegarten. Then we can walk home with Dad!" said Franny. "Alf, too."

"I suppose Alf could use an airing," said her mother. "I just don't want you to get chilled and overtired."

"I'm feeling strong. Really, I am. Please, Mom," Franny pleaded. "I'll bundle up."

Her mother knelt down and took Franny's hands in hers. "You haven't truly wanted to go outside in a long time, darling."

Franny could hear the scratch of skates on sidewalks, and the shouts on Nicholson Street, where traffic thinned out and games were played. Dusk was always the best time for games—Red Rover and Kick the Can and catch—because kids knew their time outside was limited. That made the minutes (the seconds!) as precious as emeralds. But nobody was calling for Franny to come out. They used to call for Franny all the time.

"I'm feeling strong," Franny repeated.

"All right," said her mom, standing up. "Let's go."

Alf scampered around Franny's wheelchair, his toenails clatter-ing on the hardwood floor. Suddenly he stopped to scratch vigorously behind his left ear.

"I hope that's not a flea he's after," said Nurse Olivegarten.

"Oh, I'm sure it's not," Franny said.

The Vista from Alf's Left Ear

Although he preferred the thick tangle and privacy of Alf's tail hairs when he was awake and jumping, Fleabrain liked to snooze just behind his host's left ear, where the hairs thinned out, silken and warm.

And he always got very drowsy during Alf's walks outdoors. That four-legged rhythm, *pad-paddy-pad, pad-paddy-pad*. The shifting, gorgeous kaleidoscope of color. The honks and shouts and whooshes and tweets becoming one long, humming note. A bug's lullaby.

But no, no! Mustn't sleep, he admonished himself. He must keep his eyes open, his brain alert on this wonderful outdoor jaunt. Look and listen, but not like a bug. Focus the kaleidoscope, separate the sounds. Take it all in.

He sensed Alf's excitement rising. Instinct to instinct, he, Fleabrain, must calm him!

"Streetcar's coming! Smell it, flea? Hear the clanging bells?"

"Pipe down, dog. You'll cause some trouble."

"Can't help it, flea! The dad's coming home! Supper! Oh, joy!"

"Get ahold of yourself, dog. I warn you, I'll bite!"

"OK, I'm heeling. I'm a good boy. I'm a good boy now!"

Fleabrain pitied dumb Alf so.

The dog responded only to basic threats or treats.

Life would be unbearably boring if you couldn't read or discuss books. Or discuss anything, for that matter.

Of course "dumb" was a relative term, too, not to mention a cruel one, when referring to IQ.

Franny would say that he, Fleabrain, was being critical and ungrateful to his host. She'd point out that her dog was "smart," even though he could neither talk nor read.

"Alf can shake hands!" she'd say. "Alf can roll over!"

Such puny talents, in Fleabrain's opinion. Roll over? For what purpose? A dog could roll over and roll over and roll over ad nauseam, but who benefited?

The dog! The dog got a slice of liverwurst. The dog was beside himself with joy.

The dog didn't even *know* his life was boring.

Yes, Fleabrain supposed he was jealous again. He couldn't help it. He and Alf loved the same girl.

But now . . . the red and white streetcar had arrived at the stop at the corner of Phillips and Murray, as had Franny, her mother, and Nurse Olivegarten.

Focus the kaleidoscope, Fleabrain. Separate the sounds. Enjoy the ride.

With a loud screech, the doors opened. There was the dad, descending the stairs. And there was that grouchy neighbor behind him, Gutman, Ph.D., M.D., E.R.U.D.I.T.E., or whatever the letters attached to his name were.

OK, he was jealous again, Fleabrain admitted to himself. And his pride was hurt, as well. He himself could have translated that book for Franny, even though Kafka had written a ridiculous story, in his opinion. Answers, shmancers. What answers? A man turns into a bug? No matter how hard Fleabrain put his great mind to it, he just couldn't figure out that book.

How he hated ignorance, especially his own. How he loved an intellectual challenge, as much as he relished a blood feast! He was very excited to hear the professor's views about that famous book.

"Oh, joy! Oh, joy!"

"Dog, calm yourself!"

"Can't help it, flea! WOOF!"

Revenge, Then Disaster

What happened next was all Nurse Olivegarten's fault, and Fleabrain decided to take revenge.

OK, it wasn't entirely Nurse Olivegarten's fault that Franny couldn't say one word to the imposing Professor Doctor Gutman when they all met at the streetcar stop, let alone show him *Die Verwandlung* and ask him to translate.

It was partly Alf's fault, leaping up onto the shoulders of Franny's father, knocking off his cap, which Professor Doctor Gutman bent down to retrieve. Then Professor Doctor Gutman straightened up again, and, perhaps slightly dizzy, perhaps because of the evening shadows, he didn't notice Alf's leash lying on the streetcar steps. That's when he tripped and stumbled onto the sidewalk below.

And Nurse Olivegarten really couldn't be faulted when she acted like, well, a nurse, rushing forward to help him up, yakking his ear off about ice packs for swelling and hot-water bottles for pain, flapping her long eyelashes at him. Her parents had stood over the professor, too, apologizing over and over for their dog's unruliness.

And it wasn't Nurse Olivegarten's fault that Franny had an attack of shyness and couldn't get in a single word. Professor Doctor Gutman looked so imposing in his herringbone jacket and his hat with the feather in its brim, even when he was lying flat out on the sidewalk. And then, when he stood up, brushed himself off, and scowled at everyone, it wasn't Nurse Olivegarten's fault that he'd rushed home ahead of them, or that Franny and her parents straggled far behind because it was such a steep climb along Phillips Avenue. Franny's mother said that the professor seemed too unfriendly for an invitation to Friday-night supper. Although being yakked at by everyone while lying flat out on the sidewalk would make anyone unfriendly.

All that wasn't Nurse Olivegarten's fault, but it was only Nurse Olivegarten who was bitten the next day—mercilessly.

Fleabrain's revenge! He'd really been looking forward to the professor's explanation of *Die Verwandlung* and relieved his frustration by punishing a human he detested.

If Franny's morning exercises hadn't been so uncomfortable, she herself would have giggled like crazy, especially when she saw Nurse Olivegarten scratch her bottom.

"There are fleas in this house," said Nurse Olivegarten, now pausing to scratch her earlobe.

"No one else is scratching," Franny pointed out.

Nurse Olivegarten pulled Franny's leg, hard. "My skin is particularly sensitive. And I am attractive to insects."

Nurse Olivegarten declared that as if it were a compliment. *Attractive, my foot*, thought Franny.

"Your dog has fleas, I tell you," continued Nurse Olivegarten.

"He does not!" Franny said. "He absolutely does not! How come nobody is scratching but you?"

"I suppose some people *are* more sensitive than others," said her mother.

"They say it's a certain scent emitted by a person's skin, attracting the vermin," said Nurse Olivegarten.

"Or it could be a person's imagination," said Franny.

Nurse Olivegarten held out her arm. It was peppered with small red dots. "*This* is not my imagination, young lady," she said.

"Oh, dear," said Franny's mother. "I'll have to buy some Be-Gone-with-Them."

"No!" cried Franny, sitting up. "No, no, no! Alf does *not* need flea powder!"

To Franny's horror, despite her pleas, Be-Gone-with-Them Flea Powder was applied all over Alf that afternoon. He smelled like rotting lilies, which made the entire household cough, and Alf was banished to the basement for several nights.

Fleabrain's revenge had, unfortunately, backfired.

Last Words

Fleabrain knew death was approaching.

Oh, the perils of great intelligence! If he hadn't been lost in deep thought, he could have leaped off Alf in time to escape his poisonous fate.

Now he could hardly breathe, much less leap. He heard faraway high-pitched voices singing an eerie chorus.

Poor Fleabrain. Poor, poor Fleabrain.

Darkness had quickly descended. He could no longer tell one of Alf's hairs from another. It was black as night, black as tar, black as coal. Even his ability to create decent similes had deteriorated.

How foolish of him to attack Nurse Olivegarten. Foolish, foolish, foolish! High intelligence, he was learning, did not necessarily imply common sense.

He was so tired. So cold. So, so sad.

"Oh," Fleabrain murmured. "Woe is me."

Woe is me? Were those clichéd words to be his last?

How awfully banal, compared to "It is a far, far better rest that I go to than I have ever known," penned by the English writer Charles Dickens—born February 7, 1812, died June 9, 1870—in his novel *A Tale of Two Cities*.

Or "parting is such sweet sorrow," penned by William Shakespeare in his masterpiece *Romeo and Juliet*, Act 2, Scene 2.

Or the brave words spoken by our valiant first president, George Washington—born February 22, 1732, died December 14, 1799—on *his* deathbed! "It is well, I die hard, but I am not afraid to go!"

Fleabrain wasn't confident he was going to a better rest—not at all. Also, there was nothing sweet about the parting effects of Be-Gone-with-Them, except that putrid smell. And, unlike George Washington, Fleabrain was afraid to go. Very afraid.

"Mama," he whispered.

"WOOF!" barked the overwhelmingly sweet-smelling Alf, doing his best to offer comfort.

That dog—his host, after all—wasn't so bad. His former host, that is. The guest was dying.

Oh, the shadows, the odor, the cold, cold air he couldn't seem to breathe! And that gobbledygook, which he knew was the singing of cells, atoms, nuclei, bosons, and more, taunting him in his misery. The smallest of the small, yet infinitely more powerful than he, Fleabrain, who would soon be gone forever.

Poor Fleabrain.

And then . . . Nothing.

Nothing, Then Something

Her parents took turns staying home from the shoe store to be with Franny.

But each day was essentially the same.

And each day, Franny feared the very worst for Fleabrain.

Exercises with Nurse Olivegarten, rest, meals, look out the window, read a chapter, homework, listen to the radio.

Rest.

Hope.

Peek inside the journal. Find nothing.

Exercises with Nurse Olivegarten, rest, meals, look out the window, read a chapter, homework, listen to the radio.

Rest.

Hope.

Peek inside the journal. Nothing.

Fleabrain was dead, just as they were beginning their friendship. It was all so hard to bear. Franny cried into her pillow every night.

Hope, hope.

But one day, at last!

Something.

One small word in her journal, discovered on a gray, lonely Sunday afternoon with intermittent thundershowers.

Was

The ink was pale, like a mushroom on the lawn after a rain.

Franny found herself smiling into her tomato soup at supper, so grateful that Fleabrain was still alive. At least, she hoped he was. Her smile pleased her family very much.

"Isn't the soup good, Franny?" Min said. "I helped peel off the tomato skins."

"Yes. My favorite," Franny said.

"Oh, honey, I'm glad you're feeling more like yourself again," said her mother.

Of course, those remarks would have disturbed Franny on any other day. Saint Min! Saint Min, who helped peel the tomato skins, which Franny had declined to do, peevishly, that morning.

And Franny would never, ever be "herself" again. Her real, truest, actual self, of course, was a pedestrian.

But.

That beautiful little word. *Was.* One word helped so much!

The next morning when she checked, another word had arrived in her journal.

mich

The ink was a bit darker, like strong tea with a drop of milk. But *mich*? *Mich*?

What did it mean?

Could it be in German, again, like *Die Verwandlung*?

The next morning she discovered a nearly rhyming word,

nicht

and that same afternoon, a word that didn't rhyme at all.

umbringt

Both words were written in a glossy red.

Blood red.

The hue was upsetting to Franny because of her dawning under-standing of the source of Fleabrain's "ink" and the implications for her dear Alf's comfort. Now she understood why Fleabrain's first note to her had tasted familiar when she'd impulsively eaten it. Of course, deep down, she'd probably known that blood was Fleabrain's ink of choice. His only choice, really.

On the other hand, the red was so cheerful. A ripe-strawberry red, a Santa Claus snowsuit red, a chirping cardinal red! And that could only mean one thing.

Hurrah!

Fleabrain was in top form, his appetite returned in full, though communicating (apparently) in German.

Dear Fleabrain,

I am so glad to hear from you! Get well soon.

Just so you know, I do not speak German. Or French, for that matter. But maybe someday I will.

Your friend,

Franny

Sparky's Finest

Mrs. Penelope Nelson was Franny's favorite teacher so far.

She was also a historic first, because she was the first black teacher Franny's school had ever hired. Principal Woolcott had told all the students that Creswell School was "very progressive and open-minded," and they should be proud.

Mrs. Nelson was Franny's favorite teacher, but it wasn't because she was a historic first. It was because Mrs. Nelson knew all the words to every single popular radio tune and often burst into song, just like that. And also because she traveled around the world with her anthropologist husband every summer and had stories to tell of her adventures—for instance, camel-riding in a desert sandstorm. And because she said, "Call me Penny!" to all of the Katzenbacks when she came to their home.

"Of course, *you'll* have to call me Mrs. Nelson, as soon as you get back to school," she said with a smile and a wink at Franny.

Mrs. Nelson was a newlywed, another reason Franny liked her

so much. She enveloped everyone near her in an aura of joyous optimism, as well as the scent of English Lavender by Yardley.

Mrs. Nelson came to the Katzenback home every Monday afternoon for two whole hours. She explained everything clearly, corrected every piece of homework, and made Franny feel as if she weren't missing anything at all, academically, at least.

"You will be right in the swing of things when you return to fifth grade, as if you haven't been gone one day."

Franny asked Mrs. Nelson if she knew how to translate German, since she'd done so much traveling.

"German? Nope. Not one word of it," said Mrs. Nelson. "Spanish, yes. And a bit of Tupi, believe it or not, because hubby and I will be traveling to the Brazilian rain forest this summer. Why do you ask?"

"I've been looking at some of my parents' old books," said Franny.

Mrs. Nelson let out a long whistle. "Whoo-ee! I'm impressed! But maybe you're a little too young for those books?"

"I read lots of books for my own age, too," Franny assured her.

"Well, I say this calls for a Nat King Cole song," said Mrs. Nelson.

"And then someday they may recall
We were not too young at a–a–ll!"

Still, it was a long week from Monday to Monday.

Most afternoons, Franny sat on her porch, waiting for the Pack to stroll by from wherever they'd been having fun, before they went home for supper and homework.

"Hi, Franny! See you, Franny! We miss you, Franny!" they'd call.

One day they were carrying sacks and peering at the ground, looking for discarded bottle caps before the winter snows came. The Pack shared a large bottle-cap collection, which they planned to donate to a museum at some point, or maybe even sell for cash. They kept it in the basement of Teresa's house, spread out on the concrete floor. It was most likely the largest collection of its kind, they figured, as they'd been collecting bottle caps for seventeen months. Seymour had actually been collecting on his own for two years, until Franny had once pointed out that a large joint collection made much more sense.

Teresa and her sister Rose waved at Franny. Seymour, A, B, and C were too involved in their search to look up.

"Heigh-ho!" Walter Walter called to her in a fake jolly voice. He anxiously touched the front of his shirt, where, underneath, Franny guessed, his garlic-bud necklace was hidden.

"Guess what, Franny? I found three cola caps!" cried Rose.

Teresa smiled at her younger sister. They all knew that little Rose hadn't yet mastered the concept of rarity versus quantity. Teresa herself had once been lucky enough to find a rare Red Ribbon Beverage bottle cap at the curb in front of Sol's Ye Olde Candy Shoppe. Someone had dug deep into the store's cooler and most likely pulled out the last bottle of its kind. Others had found an old Vernors Ginger Ale cap and caps for Gateway club and cherry soda pop. All the caps were certainly over five years old, if dirt and rust were any determination of age. And one Saturday, Walter Walter and Seymour (each claimed to have spotted it first) plucked an Iron City Beer cap from an overturned garbage can. Seymour insisted it was from pre–Civil

War days. Franny pointed out that they had probably used corks, not bottle caps, way back then. But Seymour said it was probably pre—one-war-or-another, so they kept it, anyway.

Franny had been hoping to discover her own rarity that autumn.

Impossible now, of course.

"Oh, Rose! Good for you," Franny called. "I bet those cola caps are beautiful."

Rose was little, but she was quick. Before anyone could stop her, she shot across Shady Avenue and up the stairs to Franny's porch. She'd remembered to look both ways before crossing but forgot that Franny was supposed to be contagious.

"Take a look," said Rose.

Across the street, Teresa was yowling like a cat. "NO-O-o-o, Rose!"

Franny leaned forward and held out her hand. Rose dropped the cola caps into Franny's cupped palm, and Franny touched them, one by one, with the tip of her finger.

"A super-duper addition to the Collection," Franny said.

"I know," said Rose, reaching for them.

"ROSE!" shrieked Teresa, racing across the street.

Teresa was known for her shrieks, a peculiar source of pride. With the proper training, operatic singing was in her future, she liked to tell everyone. Franny was used to Teresa's shrieks. But this partic-ular shriek was so vehement, it startled Franny. The three cola caps fell from her hand, skipping down the stairs.

"Roseyouarenottotouchthosecolacapsdoyouhearme!" shrieked Teresa. "Don'tyoudarethey'recoveredwithGERMS!"

"I'm not contagious!" Franny shrieked back.

"You are, too!"

"I'm not! I'm not! And very soon I'll be walking again. I'll be back in the swing of things. You'll see!"

By this time Teresa was sitting on Rose's bottom, who was struggling to reach the scattered cola caps on the front walk. Rose's shrieks, because apparently volume ran in the family, were almost as loud as her sister's.

"I want those bottle caps! I found them! They're mine!"

"She touched them!"

"I want those caps!"

"Rose, if you don't stop this, I'm going to tell everybody your big secret! I swear! I will!"

At that, Rose stopped her thrashing about but not her howling. Teresa stayed put on top of her.

All of a sudden, glowering, grumpy Professor Doctor Gutman was standing over the sisters. His black bristly eyebrows (not the kindly variety, like Sister Ed's) were raised in mighty disapproval.

"What is this ruckus?" Professor Doctor Gutman said. He turned to Teresa. "You're bigger than she is, young lady."

Professor Doctor Gutman's deep, rumbly voice sounded like a king's, or an army troop commander's. Rose quieted mid-howl. Teresa stood up, then kicked the bottle caps to the curb.

Walter Walter and Seymour Walter moseyed across the street to witness the action.

"Life is too short for angry roughhousing." Professor Doctor

Gutman's *r*'s sounded gravelly and moist, as if they were coming from deep inside of him.

"Hey, where were you born, anyway?" asked Seymour.

"In Prague, a beautiful city in Czechoslovakia," Professor Doctor Gutman replied. His eyes were bright and blue, like the European mountain lakes Franny had seen in her geography book, *Earth and Its Continents*. But his eyes were sad, too. Franny realized he'd been sad, not grouchy, all those other times she'd seen him.

"Wait a minute!" said Seymour. "That's enemy territory!"

"It used to be occupied territory, yes," said Professor Doctor Gutman. "But that war is over. And its people aren't your enemy."

All of a sudden Seymour looked fierce, as if the sound of his own voice had made him brave. "My parents said you're probably a spy."

The rest of the Pack sucked in their breaths at Seymour's rudeness.

"And not even a doctor," Seymour continued.

"I am not a practicing physician, no," said Professor Doctor Gutman, smiling politely. "I am a researcher. And I am happy to be in America."

"You have your own lab?" Walter Walter asked. "With rats and graph paper and all that?"

"It's not my own lab, and we use monkeys for our experiments, not rodents," said Professor Doctor Gutman. "We have been known to use graph paper, however."

"Researchers are just another kind of doctor, Seymour," said Walter Walter.

"Pipe down, noodlehead," said Seymour, shoving his brother's shoulder.

Teresa was still holding her wriggling sister by the arm. Rose was eyeing the bottle caps at the curb. "Well, we've got to go home now. See you, Franny," she said.

"So do we," said Seymour. "Come on, Wal."

Walter Walter glanced up at Franny on the porch. "Well, see you."

"See you," said Franny softly as Walter Walter raced up the street.

She wanted to do more than just see him. She wanted to zoom down the block with him, up and down and around and around the block, her heart thumping and her hair flying and her shoes skimming the sidewalk as if she were about to fly away.

Like Before. And she would. She would!

"Now we can breathe again," said Professor Doctor Gutman. He sat down on the steps of the Katzenback front porch, removed his hat with the feather in it, and ran a hand through his dark hair. "Gone is the Garlic Brigade."

Those rumbling *r*'s again.

"We haven't been formally introduced," he said. "My name is George Gutman."

"Very pleased to meet you. I'm Franny." Franny had her journal and *Die Verwandlung* on her lap. She'd actually also been waiting for Professor Doctor Gutman to pass by, on his way home from the streetcar stop. "By the way, a friend of mine told me about this book," she said, showing him *Die Verwandlung*. "But I can't read it, because it's in German. Do you know German, by any chance?" she asked.

"I do," he said.

"What does *Die Verwandlung* mean?"

Professor Doctor Gutman glanced at the horrifying book jacket. "*Die Verwandlung* means 'The Metamorphosis,' or, simply put, 'the change.' But why would your friend want you to read this book? It is not a book for a child."

"Many people seem to think Kafka has the answers," Franny said. She leafed through the pages to find the margin comments, then held up the book. "My friend didn't really like the story, but he wanted my opinion."

Professor Doctor Gutman smiled at the comments. "Tell your friend I agree with him. This is a silly story about a man who wakes up one morning to discover he's changed into a big bug. Kafka doesn't explain why, and, I'm sorry to tell you, I myself don't understand it, in any language. Kafka, the author, had more questions than answers."

"Oh," said Franny. "That does sound silly."

Questions? She had questions, too! Everybody had questions. But nobody seemed to have an answer. Or a cure. Tears came to her eyes. She blinked them away quickly, hoping Professor Doctor Gutman hadn't noticed.

"Well, what about this, then?" Franny flipped through the pages of her journal until she came to the mysterious little beige, brown, and red words scattered across the page.

Was

      mich

nicht

        umbringt

Professor Doctor Gutman read the words, then whispered something that sounded like a small sneeze.

Nee-cheh.

"I'm sorry?" said Franny.

"Nietzsche," said Professor Doctor Gutman. "He was a German philosopher, and these words seem to be part of one of his pronouncements." He raised his bushy eyebrows. "My, my. Your friend has been doing some advanced reading lately!"

"He's extremely intelligent and well educated," said Franny. "Self-educated."

"Well, I think your friend was sharing Nietzsche's statement *Was mich nicht umbringt, macht mich stärker.* Which, when translated, means 'What doesn't destroy me, makes me stronger.' Has he been through some rather hard times lately?"

"Oh, boy, has he ever!" said Franny. "But you say he's stronger now?"

"Your friend is saying that. Or at least he's quoting Nietzsche, who suggested that possibility."

Franny clapped her hands. Her whole body tingled with joy. "That's such good news! Stronger!"

Professor Doctor Gutman grinned. He had a gold front tooth to match his gold ring. In fact, as the sun set, Franny noticed a golden tinge at the edges of everything.

"You work with Dr. Jonas Salk, right?" asked Franny. "Everyone says he lives in the neighborhood, but nobody ever sees him because he's working so hard to conquer polio. Actually, some kids joke that he's a figment of everyone's imagination."

"He exists," said Professor Doctor Gutman. "And, yes, he does work hard. Everyone on his research team does."

Franny was relieved, as she, too, had wondered whether the great Dr. Jonas Salk truly existed. "Well, I hope we win the battle against polio," she said.

"I hope we win the battle, too," he said.

She wanted to ask him more questions about his work in the lab with Dr. Salk, but Professor Doctor Gutman had already unfolded his long legs from the stairs and was turning toward the front walk.

"Well, here is something interesting!" he said, bending down. Near the toe of his polished leather shoe was a bottle cap. "This one must be for you," he said, handing it to Franny.

The bottle cap, larger than any other, was rimmed all around in bright gold. But its center was made of glass, so that the about-to-drinker would have a magnified view of all the bubbles, like luminous marbles swimming up from the bottom of the bottle. *Sparky's Finest* was etched in curly script around the bottle cap's rim. Franny had never seen anything like it.

"How beautiful!" she said.

Her own autumn rarity.

"Nee-Cheh"

Great minds think alike, thought Fleabrain, quoting his favorite philosopher, Anonymous. He was relieved that Professor Doctor Gutman had shared his literary opinions about *Die Verwandlung*.

Fleabrain rubbed a tarsus under his "chin" pensively.

What doesn't destroy me, makes me stronger.

Nee-cheh. So that's how you pronounce it! Couldn't Friedrich Wilhelm Nietzsche—born October 15, 1844, died August 25, 1900—have done his worldwide fans a favor by spelling his name phonetically?

What doesn't destroy me, makes me stronger.

Yes, he, Fleabrain, was stronger than ever. And getting even stronger. *Stronger* wasn't even the word for it! What incredible superflea powers he had now! And he couldn't wait to display them to Franny. It was necessary to return again to the First Order of Business: meeting Franny in "person."

Greetings, my dear Franny!
I am perplexed by the overuse of birds with respect to poetic simile and metaphor.

"Life is like a broken-winged bird . . . ,"
penned the eminent
American poet Langston Hughes (born February 1, 1902),
writing of one's feelings
when dreams are dashed.

In an earlier century, the American poet Emily Dickinson (December 10, 1830—May 15, 1886)

had expressed a similar fondness for ornithology.

"Hope is the thing with feathers . . . ," Emily penned.

I believe she is saying that there is hope in the world when something as lovely as a bird exists.

I offer you a paraphrase:

"Hope is the thing with tibiae, tarsi, and tubelike mouthparts."

I do realize I am taking great liberties with great genius.

True, a bird is lovely, if you like that sort of
show-offy, twittering, high-flying creature.
   But if you remember that beauty has many definitions,
I promise I will not disappoint.

I am getting stronger, but
I want to be
at the height of my powers when we meet.
   Wait for my next missive, and do NOT misplace
Sparky's Finest.

With great excitement and trepidation,
FB

III
WINTER 1952-53: ADVENTURES

The Bath

Franny's heart ached. Loneliness hurt.

She now had new leather and steel braces to support her weakened legs, and wooden crutches to help her walk. Her braces squeaked like rusty hinges when she clumped slowly around the house. Did this mean she was "independently mobile"? She didn't feel very mobile, much preferring the zip of her wheelchair, which she could now ease into from her bed, all by herself. Then again, what difference did it make when she had hardly anywhere to go?

There had only been a few snow flurries, and it still rained every now and then, but Franny felt a silent shiver in the air. Winter had arrived. Winter meant storm windows closed to the biting chill, and windows closed meant blocking out the friendly noise and bustle of Shady Avenue.

But then, one dreary Friday in mid-December, the missive appeared in her journal.

My dear Franny,
READY?
I am!
HERE ARE YOUR INSTRUCTIONS:
Set your charming alarm clock to 2:00 a.m. Saturday morning.
We will attempt another rendezvous at Alf's tail.
Bring Sparky's Finest, your handy-dandy monocle!
Yours,
FB

Franny knew she'd be too excited to fall asleep as she waited for the alarm to ring. She asked Nurse Olivegarten to help her take a bath. Baths always made her drowsy.

They were alone in the house. The movie *Lost in Alaska* with Abbott and Costello was playing at the Manor Theater, and her parents had gone to see it. They'd asked Nurse Olivegarten to stay, for "time and a half." It was the very first time her parents had gone out together alone since Franny had come home from the hospital.

Parents needed time together to rekindle their love, Franny knew. A comedy wasn't exactly romantic, but laughing together was a fine thing to do. Her parents used to go to the movies quite a bit. Before.

And Min was at an event for teenagers at the synagogue.

Nurse Olivegarten had left the bathroom to make a quick, important phone call, but Franny didn't mind. She'd never been left alone in the bath before, and it was certainly a sign of her progress.

Anyway, it was embarrassing to be naked in front of Nurse Olivegarten, even though Nurse Olivegarten was a nurse and had probably seen hundreds, maybe thousands, of naked bodies. It was good to be alone in the tub, counting the purple and pink tiles lining the bathroom walls by twos, and then by tens. Three hundred and twelve. Three hundred and twelve, just like always.

The bathwater was warm and soft, enveloping Franny like a soapy quilt. In the water, Franny felt like her old self again. No braces and crutches. No wheelchair. Just a girl floating in a bathtub. An ordinary floating girl who could, at any moment, climb out of the tub and dry off. All by herself. At any old moment, yes, she could do that.

Franny wriggled her fingers. She shrugged her shoulders. She looked down at her belly button and clenched her stomach muscles.

Then she closed her eyes. The imaginary part came next, the part when she bent her knees, and they poked up over the bathwater like two small, shiny hills. Next came the part when she stretched out her legs, then drew them up once again. And after that, she would wiggle her toes.

There.

Franny's eyes flew open.

She'd wiggled one left toe, but in real life! She was looking right at it, wiggling away. Her toe bobbed above the water, then under, then up again, like a dancing toe-fish. Or a puppet. And she, Franny, was the puppeteer!

"Nurse Olivegarten!" Franny yelled.

She could hear Nurse Olivegarten on the telephone in the hallway. "Such hanky-panky, eh?" Nurse Olivegarten was saying. "Was

Hazel wearing that silly beret? Did Billy dance the buck-and-wing?"

"Nurse Olivegarten! Come here, please!"

Franny wished her parents were home. She wanted them to be the first to see this wonderful miracle. Her toe! Her wonderful, wiggling left toe! Hope, hope, hope. What didn't destroy her, made her stronger. Fleabrain and Nietzsche had been right. Soon she'd be herself again, better than ever.

"Nurse Olivegarten!"

Now Nurse Olivegarten was listening to the other end of her conversation. "M-*mh*. M-*mh*. M-*mh*. Isn't she, though? M-*mh*. Report *that* to Emily Post! Now, tell me about the food. Rubbery chicken, I'm guessing. M-*mh*."

The other person went on for minutes and minutes. Wasn't Franny's wiggling toe more important than rubbery chicken and Billy's buck-and-wing, whatever the heck that was? Nurse Olive-garten herself would be the first to agree, especially since her professional expertise had helped make it happen.

"Nurse Olivegarten! I moved my toe!" Franny yelled, louder now.

The water was hardly warm anymore. Her fingers were wrinkly. Franny grasped one side of the big white tub and pulled herself to a sitting position. She stared at her left toe and tried to wiggle it. She tried again, glaring angrily, willing her puppet-toe to move. It didn't budge. That's when she felt the muscle spasm, like a blow to her thigh. She gasped and fell back into the water.

"Nurse Olivegarten! Please!"

The pain, the pain! It was a howling monster swimming up

from the Allegheny River and rising from the drain. Franny breathed deeply, just as she'd been told to do during a spasm, great gulps of air that didn't help at all. She tried to sit up, but the angry pain pinned her down. Purple and pink tiles shimmied on the wall. She heard the gurgle of bathwater in her ears and, from far away, the river-monster screaming and screaming.

Nurse Olivegarten burst into the bathroom. "What's all the yelling in here?"

"I have a cramp. Can't move," Franny whispered between sobs.

Nurse Olivegarten pulled her from the tub, wrapped Franny in a big pink towel, and laid her on the bathroom floor.

"Where's the cramp? Where? Stop crying like a baby, for goodness' sake!"

"Thigh," said Franny, pointing. "Here."

Bending down, Nurse Olivegarten pressed hard on Franny's thigh and massaged the spot for several minutes. "Better?"

"A bit," said Franny. Her chest was heaving, and the sobs kept coming.

"I was gone for only a few seconds! How did it happen?"

"I moved my big toe. It was like a miracle. I was trying to make it move again. And then I got the cramp. I called and called you."

Nurse Olivegarten loomed above her, suddenly grinning. "Well, now," she said. "Of course. But it was no miracle, young lady! Didn't I tell you my treatment would work, if you'd just be patient and stop fussing all the time? Didn't I?"

"Yes," Franny whispered. She wanted to get off the cold floor.

"Now," Nurse Olivegarten said. "Do we have to go potty?"

"No," Franny said, looking away in embarrassment.

"You sure? I didn't like the looks of your bowel movement this morning."

"I'm sure. But will it happen again?"

"The cramp? I have no idea."

"No, the toe. I moved it."

"Oh, the toe!" said Nurse Olivegarten, making Franny sit up and rubbing her hair with the towel. "You bet! More than the toe. But remember, it's only a toe, eh? You have a long, long way to go. It will take a fair amount of time, but I'll get you skipping around downtown Pittsburgh eventually."

Nurse Olivegarten carried Franny to her bedroom and dressed her in her pajamas.

"You were gone for more than a few seconds, you know," said Franny. "I might have drowned."

"Don't be so dramatic! Completely your imagination. I stepped out and came right back."

"Was moving my toe my imagination, too?" Franny began to cry again.

"Well, let's see," said Nurse Olivegarten. "Which toe was it? Your left?" She reached over and jerked Franny's toe hard, moving it up and down. "Now you do it. Go ahead. Do it!"

And Franny did. Not only her toe, but her entire left foot. She began laughing and crying at the same time.

Nurse Olivegarten leaned very close. She smelled of perspiration, cologne, and cigarettes. "You should be moving more than some toes. You are just not working hard enough, fighting me all the way.

Although it's my professional duty to get you well, it is exasperating to work with you. Don't you want to walk again?"

What a dumb, dumb question! Franny closed her eyes and wished with all her heart she could jump out of bed and waltz around the room. She would be singing "A Dream Is a Wish Your Heart Makes," that beautiful song from the *Cinderella* movie, a song that made her shiver with hope every time she heard it because it promised that dreams could come true.

No matter how your heart is grieving
If you keep on believing

Grieving. Believing. A surprising rhyme. A perfect rhyme. No matter how frightened and unhappy she felt, she would never give up!

Franny opened her eyes. "I'll try to work harder, I promise. I do want to walk again."

"Well, I hope I can stay long enough to make that happen," said Nurse Olivegarten. Her olive eyes narrowed. "But my patience is wearing very thin."

The Meeting

Franny was dreaming of Nurse Olivegarten's "Patience," a thin, dingy shawl full of gaping holes. Nurse Olivegarten poked her nose through one of the holes, flaring her nostrils. "See?" Nurse Olivegarten cackled. "My Patience is wearing thin! Wearing thin! And you'll never, ever dance the buck-and-wing as well as I!"

Ludwig van Beethoven's *Moonlight Sonata* tinkled in Franny's ear. Nurse Olivegarten wrapped her torn shawl around her shoulders and began to dance. Her long legs jerked like a giant marionette's, each foot pointing in a different direction. It was not a pretty sight. Even Alf whined in annoyance—and that's when Franny woke up.

The cheerful ballerina in a sparkly, flared tutu was dancing on the face of Franny's alarm clock, endlessly inspired by the *Moonlight Sonata.* The dancer never moved her graceful arms, held high above her head, but her leaping legs and pointed toe shoes kept excellent time. Now the toe shoe of her bent leg pointed toward the two, while the toe shoe of her outstretched leg pointed toward the twelve.

Franny reached over, clicked off the musical alarm, and turned on her bedside lamp.

Alf clambered across the bed to her. He licked Franny's face, his tail wagging furiously.

"Come closer, Alfie," said Franny. "Lie down and let me look at your tail."

Alf was an intelligent mutt. He understood many words. *Come*, *Lie down*, and even *Tail* were among them. But the manner in which he showed his bottom to Franny at that moment had a specific purpose to it. He was not merely following her command. He was acting out a mission.

Franny secured the bottle cap behind one lens of her eyeglasses like a monocle, then closed her other eye and focused on Alf's hairy tail. The hairs seemed to leap out at her, each one as thick as a tulip's stem. It was as if she were looking through a powerful microscope. Closer still, and they thickened into brown, sturdy twigs.

And there he was, clinging to one of them.

Fleabrain.

He waved a long, shapely hind leg. His flat body shone in the lamplight, as brown and polished as the leather of the most expensive shoes from Katzenback's Footwear. Sparky's Finest apparently magnified sound waves, too, and when Fleabrain spoke, his voice was small, but Franny heard him clearly. Her ears tingled. Fleabrain's voice was pleasant, like the ringing of chimes.

"Franny," said Fleabrain. He sighed a high-pitched sigh. "Franny. Franny. Franny. My first word heard by human ears. A word as lovely as *Ophelia* or *Juliet* or any other name penned by Shakespeare."

"My full name is Francine," Franny said. "But everyone calls me Franny."

"I am not everyone," Fleabrain said. "For that reason, I'll call you Francine. Even lovelier."

"But how do I know you're real?" Franny asked.

Fleabrain crossed several of his six legs and leaned back comfortably upon his hair hammock. "Oh, Francine, I have so longed for a conversation such as this with you! As the French philosopher René Descartes, born March 31, 1596, died February 11, 1650, has written, '*Je pense, donc je suis*'!"

"I don't speak French," Franny said. "I think we've discussed this before."

"Right," said Fleabrain. "My sincerest apologies. Bug it! My memory is usually as sharp as a bee's stinger, but I suppose I'm in quite a tizzy, meeting you for the first time. '*Je pense, donc je suis.*' Translation: 'I think, therefore I am.' I also expound, argue, sing a cappella, compose an elegy, recite an ode, and solve algebraic equations. As well as jump incredibly high and drink blood. Therefore, I am."

"Well, I'm glad *you* know you're real," said Franny crossly. It was 2:15 A.M., and her head hurt. "But how do *I* know you are?"

"Oh, bug it. I suspected you'd ask that. I hate to do this to you, but—"

Fleabrain leaped gracefully from Alf's hair onto Franny's arm. Six small bites and the job was done—bites on Franny's arm in the shape of a tiny *F*, an exact replica of Fleabrain's distinctive signature.

"I can do the *B* for *Brain* if you need more convincing," he said, jumping back into his hair nest. "I'm sure you recognize the penmanship. Or 'mouthmanship,' as it were."

Fleabrain laughed, then stopped abruptly in mid-giggle.

"Don't worry, Francine. I used one of my gentlest venoms. The bites shouldn't itch for long, but they will still be there as proof at daybreak, before they fade away in a day or two."

"That's OK," Franny said. "I just needed to be sure."

"And don't worry about Alf. I only need a repast from my host every fortnight to stay alive these days. Sometimes less. I seem to be getting most of my nourishment from books. Much more fulfilling, not to mention slimming."

As if on cue, Alf jumped from the bed to scratch his left hind leg vigorously with his right one.

"This week's supper," explained Fleabrain. "Dogs don't really mind a mild itch, as long as they can reach it to scratch. Did you ever watch a dog scratch an itch? I mean, *really* watch? They smile as they do it!"

"That's true," said Franny, smiling herself.

"I must say, I've grown quite fond of Alf," said Fleabrain. "I'm learning to appreciate his generosity, and his pragmatic, down-to-earth attitude toward life. And, of course, the friend of my friend is my friend, to paraphrase the ancient proverb 'the enemy of my enemy is my friend.' There is some quibbling as to whether that proverb is of Arab or Chinese or Indian provenance, although all cultures eventually discover similar truths, I have learned. In any case, I do prefer my paraphrase. The dog and I are pals."

"I'm really glad about that," Franny said.

Fleabrain's charming personality radiated fellowship and kindness. These qualities made him handsome to Franny—maybe not by Hollywood standards, but who cared about that? And not having met many—or, in fact, any—other fleas up close, Franny couldn't compare him to his peers. But something told her he'd taken some pains with his appearance. The burnished, overlapping plates on his body shone, and the many hairs on his back seemed combed carefully into place.

"I have to admit, I have rather an agenda tonight. Have you any other plans?" Fleabrain asked.

"Plans?" It seemed to Franny she hadn't had "plans" in a long, long time and wouldn't have any in the near future, now that winter had arrived. "What kind of plans?"

"I would like you to meet another friend of mine. You've actually met, but I'd like you to get to know one another on a different level, both literally and figuratively speaking. And"—with a front leg, Fleabrain covered his mouthparts shyly—"I'd like you to meet some adopted members of my family," he said.

"Oh, no!" cried Franny.

"Forgive me, forgive me," said Fleabrain. His tibiae shook with embarrassment. "I've been too forward. OK, I won't subject you to my family, adopted or otherwise. This is our very first conversation, and already I'm treating you as an intimate. But I do feel as if we've been friends forever."

"It's not that," said Franny. "I would love to meet your family! I mean no offense, Fleabrain. But if my mother finds out there's been another flea infestation in the house, she'll start spraying again with Be-Gone-with-Them."

Fleabrain leaped with joy. "You'd love to meet my family? Huzzah! Franny, I give you my word of honor. I am the sole flea in this house, as far as I'm aware. My 'people' live elsewhere in the neighborhood. If you've no other plans, we can leave right away on our adventure. To celebrate your toe and foot wiggles this evening!"

Franny giggled. "'Leave right away'? Haven't you noticed? I still can't walk."

"Not a problem," said Fleabrain. "We'll bring your wheelchair."

Franny giggled again, then began to laugh harder. She fell back onto her pillow, gasping for breath. It felt wonderful to laugh like that. She was happy to know she still could.

She felt a bit light-headed, and suddenly she realized she was levitating several inches above her sheets, then floating sideways. She seemed to be headed toward her wheelchair, parked at the side of her bed.

Franny dropped gently into a seated position in the wheelchair. The yellow afghan from her bed drifted toward her, then wrapped itself around her shoulders and across her lap.

"I'll be right back," said Fleabrain.

Floating snake-like above her head, Franny's red winter cap and matching scarf soon appeared, which Fleabrain had retrieved from the hall closet.

"There!" she heard him say, his tinny voice slightly muffled by the scarf as he wound it around Franny's neck. "Comfy?"

"How . . . ?"

"*Was mich nicht umbringt, macht mich stärker,*" said Fleabrain. "'What doesn't destroy me, makes me stronger.' Not to belabor the point, but one could also opine: 'What fire doesn't destroy, it hardens,' in the words of my favorite Irish playwright and author, Oscar Wilde, born October 16, 1854, died November 30, 1900. I'll explain in greater detail soon. Whew! My exertions have left me a bit out of breath. And I still have to get you out the window."

Fleabrain hopped to the sill, raised the large window, then jumped down to the floor beneath the wheelchair. Franny grasped the arms of the chair as she was lifted, chair and all, and carried over the windowsill to the other side. She and the wheelchair landed on the lawn with a gentle thump. Alf followed.

The night sky blazed with red and orange flames from the J & L Steel Mill on the banks of the Monongahela. Street lamps glowed up and down Shady Avenue.

"We'll go for a little jaunt around the neighborhood. Follow the dog!" Fleabrain yelled from Alf's tail.

A Ride in the Night

Their route was winding and hilly. Fleabrain alternated his position between Alf's tail and Franny's shoulder. When they came to a particularly hilly section, she could feel Fleabrain push and accelerate her chair. Going down, he helped brake the speed. It was as if she were perched atop the Pippin at Kennywood Park, bumping and whizzing along. Of course, Franny didn't scream her head off, as she used to do on that roller coaster. Before. Now she just sat back and enjoyed the ride, all the dips and turns in the bracing night air.

After a while it began to seem unfair to have Fleabrain do all the work. Franny began pushing the wheels herself at the uphill mounts, to make things easier for the flea.

"Lovely of you to help," said Fleabrain, panting. "My strength is boundless, but I do feel the strain. The more I exercise, the more flexible my limbs will become."

"That's what Nurse Olivegarten always says. I hadn't realized my arms had become so strong."

But Franny didn't want to think about Nurse Olivegarten. She didn't want to think about exercises and the smell of hot, wet, woolen packs and being stuck in the house. She only wanted to think about this extraordinary ride in the night through the quiet streets of Squirrel Hill.

Most of the homes were darkened, their window blinds like closed eyelids. Every now and then, a loud snore and whistle erupted beyond a window. At a corner house on Hobart Street, Walter Walter's dad opened his bedroom window to throw a shoe at a yowling cat. Rolling along Phillips Avenue, she saw Teresa's mother, up late— or early, as the case may be—folding a towering pile of laundry on the dining room table. Several dogs inside their homes greeted Alf with surprised yelps, most likely inhaling the odor of Alf's excitement as he sped by. The air was cool and damp on her cheeks, but the afghan kept her warm, as did the exertion of climbing the hilly terrain, with Fleabrain's help.

Up and down, up and down, they rolled through the streets branching off Shady Avenue, finally circling back to Nicholson Street, heading toward Frick Park.

"Now that you know how strong your arms are, let's try a bigger challenge," Fleabrain said.

"Nicholson Street is very steep!" said Franny.

"We can do it." Fleabrain whistled an inspiring yet familiar tune in her ear. The sound of the wheelchair gliding smoothly up the hilly street made for a pleasant accompaniment to the music.

"You whistle very well," Franny said. "So many talents! And I recognize that tune."

"Thank you, Francine. But only the violin does this piece real justice. It's from the second movement of the Polish composer Henryk Wieniawski's Violin Concerto No. 2 in D minor. Born July 10, 1835, died March 31, 1880. Such a superb concerto! I much prefer Wieniawski's second movement to the first, don't you?" said Fleabrain.

"I guess I've only heard a snippet of the second movement," Franny said. "It's the opening theme to *The Guiding Light*, my mother's favorite soap opera on the radio."

"Oh, do have a listen to the entire recording when you can!" exclaimed Fleabrain.

They had reached the top of Nicholson at Beechwood Boulevard.

"We did it!" cried Franny.

"Of course," said Fleabrain. "Never any doubt in my mind."

Beechwood Boulevard's wide expanse was silent and empty of cars.

"Let's rest a bit and catch our breath before we cross this big street," said Fleabrain.

Fleabrain had thought of everything. Tucked in a corner at the back of her seat was a small bag of popcorn and an apple. She'd forgotten how good a sour-sweet apple tasted outdoors, crisp and chilled.

As Franny munched, Fleabrain explained as much as he could.

"It seems that a second dose of Be-Gone-with-Them, to which I was subjected, as you are well aware, has the paradoxical effect of bestowing extraordinary powers upon those who have survived a first dose. I don't know if this has ever happened. There had never before *been* any survivors of the first dose, as far as I know, although, of course, I am going by purely anecdotal evidence. But I surmise that I developed powerful antibodies, which, when fighting the poison a second time, in some way affected my resilin. Resilin is the rubbery protein in a flea's limbs, which explains my amazing jumping ability under normal conditions. My unfortunate experience with Be-Gone-with-Them helped concentrate my resilin so that it became even more effective. I didn't think I could become stronger and smarter, but here I am."

"I'm not sure I understand all that, but it sounds wonderful," said Franny.

"'Ah! Sweet Mystery of Life.' Sweet mysteries of the molecules and atoms of which we are composed. Never, ever underestimate them. Small is great, I am learning."

"*You* are great, Fleabrain," said Franny. "And kind, too."

"I meant 'great' in the 'powerful' sense," said Fleabrain, "as opposed to the 'wonderful' sense, although small *can* be wonderful, of course. Small is great. Invisible is great. The atom is great. Antibodies are great! I'm sure the German-born physicist Albert Einstein—born March 14, 1879—and I are in accord about all this, as we are about many things, although I've never quite reconciled myself to his vegetarianism. And as the Roman philosopher Lucretius—born 99 BC, died 55 BC—suggested . . ."

At this point Franny couldn't suppress a yawn, which she tried to hide with her apple core.

"Oh, dear," cried Fleabrain. "I'm prattling on and on! I just find everything so fascinating, and, before meeting you, I haven't been able to share it with anyone."

"You're not boring me, Fleabrain. I'm just sleepy and comfortable," said Franny. "Small is great. I will remember that. But what about viruses? The poliovirus, for instance."

Fleabrain paused briefly. A flea-millisecond of a pause, but Franny noticed.

"Not so great," he admitted ruefully. "Powerful, yes. But not wonderful. Anyway, let's not talk about viruses. It's time to cross the boulevard and meet a couple of fellows who are very important to me, besides yourself and Alf, of course. And do bring that apple core."

A police car from the Northumberland station was patrolling the area. Fleabrain and Franny and Alf waited until the coast was clear, hiding behind a big dark tree. Then they scurried across Beechwood Boulevard and along English Lane to the stables.

A joyful whinny soon greeted them—Lightning, stomping about in the second stall. Fleabrain unlatched the gate to the stall, as the other horses watched from theirs. The horse approached Franny, bending down, as he always did, to nuzzle her neck.

"For you," said Franny, giving him the apple core. "Dear Fleabrain thought of everything."

Meanwhile, Fleabrain had delved into Lightning's tail and the area around the horse's bottom. "Over here, Francine," he called in a muffled voice. "Come meet some friends of mine."

On close inspection with Sparky's Finest, and by the light of the gleaming moon, Franny could see Fleabrain leaping and cavorting with several tiny multilegged insects, who seemed very excited to see him. "I visit the ticks as often as I can," said Fleabrain, "whenever Alf takes this particular route. Unfortunately, a few of these cute tykes will be dead by tomorrow."

"Oh, no!"

Fleabrain sighed. "Well, *c'est la vie*. Excuse me; translation from the French: 'such is life.' Or such is the life cycle of the ordinary tick. Very, very short. I'm the stablest, most constant part of their lives. They like to tell me old tales they've heard of my father, one lonely flea wandering among their own tick ancestors, long, long ago, before he jumped onto Alf's tail to join my mother. 'Long ago' in relative terms, of course, considering their short lives. I think of them as my adopted family. To them, I am their dear Uncle Fleabrain."

"Fleabrain, you are so kind and good and generous. I am very, very glad to know you, especially in person."

"Well . . ." Fleabrain covered the sides of his face with his front legs, where Franny supposed his eyes were, but they were so tiny, she could hardly see them, even with Sparky's Finest. "This is embarrassing to admit, but since we've met in 'person,' I'm realizing I have to be honest with you. If we're going to be true friends, that is." His breath caught in a sob.

"Fleabrain, what's wrong?" Franny asked.

"Oh, it's Charlotte. It's always Charlotte, bug it!"

"You mean Charlotte, the spider from *Charlotte's Web*?"

"Of course I mean *that* Charlotte! Who else?"

"I don't understand . . ."

"I could never fathom her appeal, quite frankly. But after pondering on it, I sense she is lovable for her motherly quality toward all. So I wanted you to know that I've got some of that quality, too.

Up you go, kiddies! Uncle Fleabrain will give you a ride!" Fleabrain bounced several ticks on his back boisterously—a difficult task, since they were larger than he was. "I've actually learned to enjoy myself around these young 'uns."

"Charlotte was and is an inspiration to all, I agree," said Franny.

"I guess," said Fleabrain grudgingly.

"And, Fleabrain, I can easily tell that you are a terrific uncle."

Fleabrain's body plates turned an even darker color of brown, which Franny assumed was an embarrassed but happy blush. "Thanks," he said.

Lightning whinnied, as if wondering why they were paying more attention to the back of him than the front.

At that, Fleabrain gently dislodged a young tick from his back and took a giant leap forward, landing in Lightning's straggly mane. "Now, for the other reason we are here—the most exciting reason, as a matter of fact! Equestrian delights!"

FB Saliva #1

After affixing Lightning's famous old racing saddle and reins, Fleabrain helped Franny mount sidesaddle, then gently maneuvered her legs across the saddle and into the stirrups.

"The idea came to me while reading the medical views of the ancient Greeks," said Fleabrain. "Especially Hippocrates, born 460 BC, died 377 BC. 'Riding's healing rhythm,' and all that. He was one smart doc, that Hippocrates."

"I've never ridden a horse," Franny admitted, shivering with excitement.

Fleabrain tied the yellow afghan like a cloak around Franny's shoulders.

"Lightning will take care of you—don't you worry. His forebears, once companions to the gods, were taught to know and love the human soul. But first, an application of FB Saliva #1, for speedy woof and whinny travel. My saliva is composed of minute yet immensely powerful particles invisible to the naked eye—even mine."

Fleabrain hopped from Lightning to Alf, applying his solution to their ears and limbs with a few quick bites.

"Now, heigh-ho, Lightning and Alf, away!" he called.

Old Lightning's arthritic trot was slow and tentative, as if he couldn't quite believe he was free. Not quite a "healing rhythm."

"You can do it, O noble steed!" Franny whispered.

Lightning tossed his head and whinnied, seeming to remember his godly heritage. Very soon his gait quickened to a confident gallop, following Franny's wishes without her saying or doing very much. A tiny tug of the reins, a pat on his neck, and, yes, oh yes! even a nudge with her left toe every now and then, the same toe she'd wiggled in the bathtub.

From somewhere within Lightning's streaming mane, Fleabrain whistled Wieniawski's concerto, quickening its rhythm to match the horse's percussive hoofbeats. To Franny's surprise, Alf raced at their side, not a fat and lumbering Alf but a sleeker, wolflike version of himself.

"Atta boy, Alf!" called Fleabrain.

Faster and faster they galloped upstreet toward Forbes Avenue, the warmth of Lightning's flanks against Franny's own, the wind whipping her face, the clatter of hooves pounding in her ears. How wonderful to look down from a mighty steed, rather than stare up at the world from her wheelchair!

And here was the world again! The greengrocer and the deli and the butcher shops, the chickens and ducks and salamis swaying in darkened windows; Weinstein's Restaurant; the post office; the bank. Still there! Across the street, the Manor Theater; the five-and-dime;

the Waldorf Bakery. Still there, too! At the hub of Forbes and Murray, the Gulf gas station, the newsstand, Sol's for pop, Isaly's for towering ice cream cones, shops for stylish clothes. Everything was still there, exactly as she'd pictured it in her mind for so long.

Faster and faster, and faster still! Then, with a loud whinny and a sharp woof, Lightning and Franny and Fleabrain and Alf left the sidewalks of Squirrel Hill. Up, up, up they flew, over red-hot slag heaps, great factories and steel mills, the new parkway, still a hole in a hill, west over silent and majestic parks, toward the graceful bridges whose rivers met at the Ohio. Higher and faster still, zooming back over downtown Pittsburgh's tall buildings. Even over the Gulf Tower, tallest of all! Its neon-lit pyramid top gave the nightly weather report as they whizzed over it. Flashing blue meant cold and drizzly. *Who cares?* thought Franny. *I'm warm atop my noble steed!*

"*Wheeee-ee!*" squealed Fleabrain. "*Awhooo!*" howled Alf, newly wolflike. "*Eeeeeehhh!*" whinnied Lightning nobly.

Franny was too thrilled to shout anything at all. They circled back toward the neighborhood of Oakland and the University of Pittsburgh campus. Fleabrain hollered, "Prepare to descend!"

Down they went, hovering at the bottom floors of the Pittsburgh Municipal Hospital on the campus grounds. Cigarette smoke floated from an open window. Franny leaned forward to peek inside.

There he was, working in his famous laboratory.

The great Dr. Jonas Salk.

In the flesh!

Franny recognized him right away. He looked just like his photo in the *Pittsburgh Press*—balding, bespectacled, smoking a cigarette.

He was wearing his dignified white lab coat and squinting at a large test tube, which he held aloft. And there was his team of diligent lab technicians and scientists, also hard at work at the crack of dawn, including the erudite Professor Doctor George Gutman. Some were bent over vials, some were checking notes on, yes, graph paper, still others in the basement examined the shaking incubators holding the precious mixture—the mixture that would eventually be used to conquer polio, learn its secrets, and save its victims. All were so intent on their lifesaving mission that not a single one of them noticed a dog and a horse and the horse's rider, wearing a red hat and scarf and wrapped in a yellow afghan–cloak, floating outside the laboratory window. Franny was cheered by their predawn industriousness and by the hope for prevention and cure wafting from the window with all that cigarette smoke.

"Francine, now you can say you were a witness to history in the making. Because of yours truly."

"Thank you, Fleabrain," said Franny. She'd known all along that Dr. Jonas Salk truly existed, but it felt wonderful to know for sure.

"All right, team, prepare to ascend again!" Fleabrain shouted, his voice faint against the rising wind. A light rain began to fall, just as the Gulf Tower had predicted. They headed back toward the stables, in time to witness an unexpected spectacle as daylight returned.

Two masked robbers, each carrying a bulging sack of cash, raced from Peoples Bank on Forbes Avenue. One burly man waited by a getaway car. Then two robbers and one burly lookout–man fainted dead away on the wet sidewalk, having spotted the equestrian Franny and her friends zooming overhead. Franny could hear sirens as police cars raced to the scene.

"Superflea and Francine, the Girl of Steel! Champions of Truth, Justice, and the American Way! Our size belies our strength. Heigh-ho, Alfie and Lightning, away! Now we can go home, our mission completed for today," exulted Fleabrain. "I've always admired the moral compasses of Superman and the Lone Ranger, fictional though they may be. Such fine examples of popular culture."

At the stables again, Fleabrain helped Franny down from the horse into her chair, then wrapped her in the afghan for the ride home. And Lightning, who would keep their secrets safe, always and forever, trotted back to his stall for breakfast.

What the Professor Knew

George Gutman knew his work was important, and he loved it.

He loved the sound of the busy, churning canisters in the basement, and the clean smell of the laboratories above.

He loved the lab's monkeys in their second-floor cages, many of whom would die for a noble cause. He loved the elegant chain of events the monkeys represented: Salk's scientific theories made real by patience and hard work!

Kidney cells were extracted from the monkeys.

The kidney cells were then used to harvest the poliovirus, large quantities of it, in churning canisters.

The poliovirus was killed with formaldehyde.

The inactive virus was made into a vaccine.

The vaccine was given to monkeys.

And then the inoculated monkeys were exposed to the dangerous poliovirus.

Did those monkeys develop antibodies, disease-fighting agents against polio, after receiving the vaccine? Yes!

Did the vaccine protect them against polio? Yes, most of the time.

Over and over again the chain of events was repeated; day after sixteen-hour working day, six days a week, the search for a perfectly safe and effective vaccine continued.

He even loved the smell of Salk's cigarettes, because he loved his hardworking boss, although he did think his boss smoked too much.

And the professor knew that he loved his work even more, lately, because of that young girl with polio in his neighborhood. Annie? Fanny? He should find out her name again. Names were important. There were so many others like her. There were others who would become like her. That's why his work was necessary. Time was of the essence, to create the lifesaving vaccine.

But he also knew that this girl was unusual. Many were stricken with polio, but how many of them tried to read Franz Kafka? Kafka's stories were for adults, difficult and strange. They didn't make sense.

The professor knew what the girl's question for Kafka would be, if Kafka were still alive.

"Mr. Kafka, how come some people get polio and others don't? That doesn't make sense," she would ask.

The professor knew that Kafka would have answered with more questions, because Kafka wouldn't have an answer.

"Young lady, who knows?" Kafka would ask, his dark eyes flashing with a gleeful anger. "Why ask me? Am I a scientist? And who says life itself has to make sense? If you wake up one morning as a bug, does that make any less sense than the world's wars in Europe and Korea?"

Life didn't make sense to the professor. Once, he'd had a wife and a daughter, and they'd all lived together in a faraway European city. His daughter, blue-eyed and long-limbed, had loved books, just like his young neighbor on Shady Avenue. And buttered noodles with poppy seeds, and marionettes, and her clarinet, and her grandfather's horse.

Why, just today, from the corner of his eye, the professor had seen a reflection in the windowpane at the first light of morning. There was his daughter on that horse, riding home to him across a snowy field. Of course, it was only the professor's mind playing a little trick on him. He'd been working too hard. His daughter had died in a concentration camp in a senseless war, as had his wife. Nameless and alone.

And it didn't make sense that this young neighbor should also feel alone, imagining herself waking up as an ugly, unwanted bug, that *Ungeziefer* in Kafka's story. A beautiful girl, inside and out. Just like his daughter, Sophie, had been. Sophie Harriet Gutman.

They must find the right vaccine! Test it on more monkeys until it was absolutely perfect. And higher primates, too! Of course he would test the vaccine on himself, just as the other researchers had.

And then, the children. They must give it to all the children. But what if the vaccine gave them polio instead of protecting them? The risk was there. That was why he and Salk would keep working sixteen hours a day, six days a week, until the perfect vaccine was developed.

Blisters

T he six little bites on Franny's arm in the shape of a distinctive *F* were fading by early Sunday morning, as Fleabrain
had promised. They had hardly itched at all. She was careful to keep the bites hidden from her family, but that was easy to do.
Their house was always drafty and chilly in the winter, and knitted,
long-sleeved sweaters were necessary indoors. She was sorry to
see Fleabrain's bites fade, since they were a reminder of their time
together. Already the memory of their ride was fading a little, too.
She tried to re-create it, tightening her thighs, reaching out with her
arms, pulling imaginary reins this way and that, and tapping with her
toe, the one that moved. Of course, it wasn't the same.

Still, Franny felt a new joy blooming like a winter petunia inside
of her. Was there such a thing as a winter petunia? A soft-petaled but
determined petunia, pushing itself up through the snow.

She was especially joyous because Nurse Olivegarten had called
in sick with the sniffles. Next Thursday would be Christmas Day, and
Nurse Olivegarten would be off then, too, and Friday and the next

Saturday. Four Nurse Olivegarten–less days to look forward to. And whenever the nurse wasn't around, Franny removed her hated leg braces and special, ugly, clodhopper shoes.

The winter petunia inside of her was her beautiful secret. She hadn't told anyone yet about her toe and ankle wiggle. Surprisingly, Nurse Olivegarten hadn't, either. If her parents and Min had known, they'd be hollering with joy! She would tell them herself, when the time was right. Maybe she'd wait until she could stand up and skip right across the room.

It was reading time at the Katzenbacks', just as it usually was on Sunday mornings. Another reason to be happy. Even Before, the whole family had read together, the clock ticking cheerfully on the mantel, opera on the radio, a beet borscht on the stove warming the whole house. Min and Franny used to go to the library together, hopping onto the streetcar to the Oakland Branch, sometimes visiting the grand Carnegie Museums, as well. Or they'd bring home a stack of books from the new neighborhood bookmobile. Before. Nowadays Min went alone, bringing books home for Franny and herself.

Her parents traded sections of the morning newspaper.

"Bank robbery at Peoples Bank at dawn yesterday," said Mr. Katzenback. "Page four."

"Oh, no!" said Mrs. Katzenback.

"Don't worry. Police got 'em," said Mr. Katzenback, shaking the newspaper and turning the page.

"BANK ROBBERS ARRESTED!" screamed the headline.

"Our tax money is doing some good," said Mrs. Katzenback.

Franny bent her head over her book, hiding her grin. "Heigh-ho,

Franny, away!" she said softly. At her feet, Alf snorted, giving a quick scratch to his hindquarters.

"Why did you ask for so many books about horses this week, Fran?" Min asked.

"Why not? I happen to like horses," said Franny.

She was already one-third of the way through *My Friend Flicka*. Piled up by the side of her wheelchair were her other library books. *The Black Stallion. Black Beauty. The Red Pony.* Franny loved the feeling of having a pile of books waiting for her.

Her mother and Min glanced at each other across the room.

"I know what you two are thinking," Franny said. "You're thinking I'm never going to get a chance to ride, so why am I bothering to read about horses?"

"I was thinking no such thing," said her mother.

"Ha!" said Franny. She had known her mother her entire life, and she knew exactly when Muriel Katzenback was fudging the truth. She usually twitched her nose sideways to the left, and her mother had done just that.

"I have no problems with horseback riding, under extremely careful supervision," said Mrs. Katzenback. "But we don't live on a farm in the country."

"We don't plan on becoming stage performers, either, but that didn't stop us from taking tap-dancing lessons," said Franny. "Min, next time please get me some books on tap dancing."

"Oh, Franny," said Saint Min. "You don't even like tap dancing."

Min was right. Last year they'd both signed up for Sunday Tap

Time at the Gene Kelly Studio of the Dance. Franny had quit after one week. Min had quit after two. They'd both agreed that tap dancing was the stupidest thing. *Shuffle, shuffle, clickety-clack.* Just the stupidest thing! And so were those black, noisy shoes tied with huge, floppy bows that kept getting untied. Tap dancing had seemed like a good idea at the time. Dancing lessons were much cheaper than piano lessons, and, anyway, they couldn't afford a piano. And other kids in the Pack were taking tap. But Franny and Min had no idea how terrible it was until they tried it.

"Those awful shoes!" said Min. "And remember the blister I got on my heel, as big as a dandelion head? All that gooey liquid squirting out when it burst?"

"Shuffle, shuffle, clickety-clack," said Franny, and then they were both laughing their heads off together. Just like Before.

It seemed like the perfect moment. She just couldn't keep it inside anymore. "Look, everybody!" cried Franny. She lifted her left foot up and down at the ankle. "It may not be tap dancing, but I'm wiggling my toe inside my shoe. Shuffle, shuffle, clickety-clack!"

Franny had been right about everyone's reaction. Oh, the hollers of joy! The hugs and sloppy kisses! But there were tears on their cheeks, too. In all her life, Franny had never seen her parents cry. Even when she'd first come down with polio, they'd seemed too frozen with fear to cry.

"I'm so grateful to that wonderful Nurse Olivegarten," her mother said, blowing her nose. "I'll telephone her right away. She was so right. Her treatment works!"

"Don't," said Franny. "She already knows."

Her father frowned. "I wonder why she didn't mention it. She said that her Friday evening with you had been quiet and uneventful."

"She's too modest," said Mrs. Katzenback. "She must have breakthroughs like this all the time."

A quiet and uneventful evening, my foot, thought Franny. Nurse Olivegarten didn't want to say anything about what happened, good *or* bad, and, anyway, it was just a few toes, she would say. But Franny didn't want to think about Nurse Olivegarten, especially on Nurse Olivegarten's day off. What she wanted to do was dance (even tap-dance!) and sing and soar through the air with happiness. And if she couldn't do that, she would do almost the next best thing.

Wheelies.

She'd discovered she could do them the other day, whizzing down the long hall in her wheelchair. Just as she reached the lofty bookcase at the end of the hallway, she reared backward on her wheels, neighing, *"Eeeeeeeehhhh!"* then hollering, "Heigh-ho, Franny, away!"

Up and down the hallway and back again, two times, three times, then four. *"Eeeeeeeeehhhh!"*

It felt so good.

"Franny, stop that now!" cried her mother. "You'll exhaust yourself. It's just too much for you."

"I'm riding my horse, Mama," said Franny. "You said you didn't have a problem with that."

"What your mother means is—" said Mr. Katzenback.

"I think she means I'm an invalid," said Franny. "In-valid. Ab-normal."

"You know what I think?" Min said. "I think Franny and I should both get ourselves some fresh air."

"I think so, too," said Franny. *"Eeeeeeehhhh!"* she whinnied. "Franny and Min, away!"

"It looks like rain," said their mother.

But Min was already tugging their warm jackets and hats and scarves from the hall closet before her parents could say no.

"We don't want you to get overtired, girls," said their father.

"Better than undertired!" said Franny, which made both girls laugh.

They were still laughing as Mr. Katzenback carried Franny to the lawn chair on the front porch, went back in to bring out her wheelchair, then helped Franny into it. Min pushed the wheelchair down the front walk as Mr. Katzenback followed them to the sidewalk.

"Be careful," he said, his mouth curved into a worried smile.

"You look like we're going on a long trip, Dad," said Franny. "We'll be fine."

Too bad it wasn't snowing, she thought. Then she could pretend she was the Snow Queen, rolling along in her chariot. Franny loved the beauty of the freshly fallen snow blanketing Squirrel Hill, before it was powdered over with gray soot from the mills.

Professor Doctor Gutman was coming down the street, carrying a grocery bag. Franny's heart thumped with joy and hope when she saw him. He gave them a tired smile, then tipped his hat in the fancy European way Franny recognized from movies she'd seen. She imagined hardworking Professor Doctor Gutman alone at a small kitchen table, eating a single lamb chop, his fork and knife against the plate the only sounds in the room.

"My parents would like to invite you to supper on a Friday evening," Franny blurted out. "They suggested the first Friday night of 1953. Six o'clock. We hope you can come."

"It would be my pleasure," said Professor Doctor Gutman, smiling his gold tooth at them. "Thank them for the invitation . . . Please excuse me, I've forgotten your name."

"Franny, short for Francine. And this is my sister, Min, short for Minot. French names, but we don't speak French."

"Franny. And Min. Thank you." The professor tipped his hat again in his fancy, polite way.

After he'd gone, Min asked, "Did Mom and Dad really tell you to invite him?"

"No," said Franny. "Actually, Mom thought he was too grouchy to invite to supper, but she's wrong. He's very nice. And, anyway, it's too late now."

"We'd better tell them they'll have a guest very soon," said Min, giggling.

As they went up Shady Avenue, Franny and Min began singing at the very top of their lungs. The song they sang was the best song in the world, Franny used to say when she was little. In a way, it still was.

A boy was sitting on a railroad track,
His feet were full of BLISTERS.
He tore his pants on a rusty nail,
So now he wears his SISTER'S!

Oh, it ain't gonna rain, no more, no more,
It ain't gonna rain no more.
So how in the HECK
Can I wash my NECK
If it ain't gonna rain no more?

"Oh, Franny," said Min. "I've missed you."

"Really? I didn't go anywhere," Franny said.

"You did so. Well, the goofy, happy, and friendly you went away."

Franny knew what Min meant. Today she felt more like herself again. "Listen, Min," she said. "Help me stand."

"What do you mean? You're not wearing your braces or your sturdy shoes."

"It won't matter. Help me stand up, right now. I'm feeling very strong. Maybe I can even take a few steps."

Min wrinkled her brow. "Are you sure, Fran? What if . . . ?"

"What if *what*?" asked Franny. "I'm feeling very strong, I'm telling you."

"Well, OK," said Min. She put her arms under Franny's armpits and pulled her from the wheelchair, Franny's arms around Min's neck. With great effort, Min propped up Franny against her.

"Lean on me," Min whispered.

"Just at first," said Franny. "Then I want to stand by myself."

She and Min stood hugging, and soon, slowly, slowly, Franny withdrew her arms.

"There," Franny said. She looked Min straight in the eye. They grinned at one another. "Now I'm going to move my left toe, and then my left foot. Then I'm going to move my right toe and my right foot. And then, *ta-da!* I'll walk."

"Careful," said Min.

Who needed Nurse Olivegarten? Left foot, right foot— easy-peasy.

Except it wasn't. Her left toe and her left foot refused to move. She gritted her teeth and tried again.

"Are you OK?" Min asked.

"Please. Don't help me," Franny said. She closed her eyes and tried again. *Move, move!* It was as if the ability to move had been part of a long-ago dream. The effort made her dizzy. "Give me a few seconds," she said, swaying. "There," she said, feeling some movement. "I did it."

But Min's worried gaze was no longer straight in front of her. She was looking down at Franny, because Franny was lying flat on the sidewalk.

"Oh, Franny!" Min said, her lips trembling.

Here I am, Franny thought. *This is the new real me. The always-lying-down-needing-help real me.*

And suddenly there was Teresa, looking down at her, too, and Quiet Katy, and Teresa's older sister, Jane.

Min pulled Franny into a sitting position, her hands under Franny's arms.

"Please, help me get my sister to her chair," she said to the others.

Teresa, Jane, and Quiet Katy backed away, then stood pale and still, as if frozen by a wizard's spell.

"Please," Min repeated. Franny's stiff legs made a quiet *shushing* noise as Min dragged her along the sidewalk.

"I'll help," said Quiet Katy, stepping forward, but Min had already lifted Franny into the wheelchair. She leaned her head on Franny's shoulder to rest for a few seconds.

Franny saw that Quiet Katy was holding a cloth bag, and so were the others. She knew that inside those bags were the black shoes with their floppy ribbons for Sunday Tap Time at the Gene Kelly Studio of the Dance. And she knew she'd give anything in the whole world to be walking home from the streetcar stop after Sunday Tap Time. It didn't even matter if tap dancing was the stupidest thing.

"See you, Franny," said Teresa. "Take care of yourself."

Quiet Katy walked backward, solemnly watching Franny and Min.

"That poor, poor cripple!" said Jane.

Franny knew she and Min weren't supposed to hear that.

Poor cripple.

"I'm sorry, Franny," Min said. "Let's just keep going."

Min began singing again, not at the top of her lungs this time.

A boy was sitting on a railroad track,
His feet were full of blisters.

But Franny didn't want to sing or keep going. The whole day had a blister on it now.

"No, let's go home," she said.

Holiday Headlines

Press

un...
night,
morrow,
high 34. We...

A2

Sunday, December 21, 1952

CHILDREN'S CHRISTMAS GIFTS SAVED FROM FIRE!

A fire was mysteriously extinguished by a garden hose pushed through an open living room window in the Manchester District of the North Side last night. The blaze was caused by an electrical short circuit near an illuminated, indoor Christmas tree at the home of Mr. and Mrs. Bill Jenkins and their four children. They had been visiting relatives at the time. Gifts under the tree had been moved to the dining room and left intact.

"Our neighbors reported hearing hoofbeats outside but couldn't see the rider in the dark," said Mr. Jenkins. "Our family is grateful to the firefighter or firefighters, whoever they might be."

Sunday, December 21, 1952

SURPRISE TURKEYS DELIVERED TO ST. JOSEPH'S HOUSE OF HOSPITALITY!

A clerical error resulted in St. Joseph's House of Hospitality facing a shortage of ten turkeys for its annual Holiday Happiness Feast. Roasted birds in paper bags from Weinstein's Restaurant in Squirrel Hill were left last night at the building's front door, just in time for tomorrow's feast.

When contacted by a reporter, Mr. Itzy Weinstein expressed no knowledge of the good deed, although his own turkey inventory seemed to be lower than usual.

"We respect and admire his modest- " said Father McDougall of St. Joseph's

Monday, December 22, 1952

"ANGEL" LIGHTS STAR ON GATEWAY TREE

A young equestrian dressed as an angel hovered on her horse over the Christmas tree at the recently completed Gateway Center, lighting the star candle at the giant tree's tip-top.

"I am amazed at the level of technical expertise this feat involved," crowed a proud Mayor David L. Lawrence, who was at the inaugural tree-lighting ceremony. "Have you ever seen anything like it? That's Pittsburgh's progress for you!"

Event organizers stated that a wooden mannequin descending from a wire had been initially planned for the extravaganza. "I guess the 'powers that be' were concerned about fire safety," said one.

The names of the "powers that be" who made this dazzling live event possible are unavailable at this time.

Rag un...
night,
morrow,
high 22. W...

Wednesday, December 24, 1952

NEW MUSICAL PROGRAM AT MELLON BANK THIS HOLIDAY SEASON

by Jimmy Regis, Special Correspondent

The annual holiday musical festival took place yesterday evening at Mellon Bank on Smithfield Street.

Listeners were treated to the beauteous singing of the Westinghouse Men's and Women's Choruses. The usual Christmas fare, which included a medley of carols, as well as popular tunes such as "I Saw Mommy Kissing Santa Claus," delighted the crowd.

A young soloist, the Gateway Center "angel," perched on her handsome steed in the shadows of the bank's imposing doorway, sang some Hanukkah celebratory tunes, including "The Dreidel Song" and "Ocho Kandelikas." The latter is a song in the Ladino language.

"Ladino is a Judeo-Spanish language with origins in medieval Spain," said Richard Kaufman, a Spanish teacher at Taylor Allderdice High School. In addition, a talented whistler, hidden from the audience (a dramatic touch, many agreed), spontaneously regaled listeners with the second movement of Henryk Wieniawski's Violin Concerto No. 2 in D minor. The popular radio soap opera "The Guiding Light" uses the piece for its introduction, and it "is particularly approtpriate in this spiritual context," said Elva Morris, a history teacher at Taylor Allderdice High School.

"What a varied and ecumenical treat!" crowed a proud Mayor David L. Lawrence, who attended the Mellon Bank concert.

Friday, December 26, 1952
FRANTIC FATHER DELIVERS BABY AS STORK WINS OVER SANTA!

The best Christmas gift in the world was delivered to a Beechview couple yesterday: an infant son.

"One could say delivered 'by' rather than 'to,'" declared the father, Mr. Roy Perroni, who delivered the baby himself. "It was as if a tiny flea was buzzing in my ear the whole time, telling me exactly what to do."

The new dad also described objects swooping past the Beechview couple's bedroom window. "I thought it was a flock of Christmas angels. But maybe it was a flock of storks, if storks can whinny. I know—it was Santa's reindeer!" He laughed. "Although I did hear a dog barking as well. I was seeing and hearing things under stress, I suppose."

Mother and child are resting comfortably at Allegheny General Hospital.

Truths of the Universe

Fleabrain loved the Sabbath, or *Shabbos*, as the Katzenback family called it in Yiddish, that venerable old language. Only Great-grandfather Zadie Ben and Fleabrain spoke and understood Yiddish fluently; the rest of the family knew a few words here and there. Fleabrain had learned the language while reading the work of the fine Yiddish poet Rosa Harning Lebensboym, born 1887, died 1952.

And Fleabrain loved when the Katzenbacks invited guests, which always resulted in lively and provocative conversation. That night, the first Friday of 1953, there were three guests besides Zadie Ben, who was visiting from his nursing home: Professor Doctor Gutman, Nurse Olivegarten, and Penny Nelson, Franny's teacher, whose husband was out of town attending to his anthropological affairs.

"This is my first *Shabbos* meal!" said Penny, who wasn't of the Jewish faith.

"Our family is delighted to have you at our Sabbath table," said Mrs. Katzenback.

One could say that Fleabrain was also a member of the Katzenback family, although only one member of that family would agree. But there they were, he and Alf, at the *Shabbos* table. OK, under the table. And both were praying in their own way, as were the eight humans above them.

Alf was praying that challah bread crumbs and other delicacies would drop to the floor. A stray carrot coin, a fat noodle, or a smidgen of chicken from the soup. Alf hoped Franny and Min would answer his prayers, and they did.

As it should be, thought Fleabrain. *The old dog deserves those little extras.*

"More, more!" whined Alf.

Fleabrain clasped his hairy front legs together in a prayerful attitude. But he couldn't think of anything to ask for. He had it all! Two best friends (although one was more of a generous host). A warm, hairy bed. The occasional blood feast. Stimulating reading materials. Adventure. His health.

Was there more in life to be had?

He supposed he should give a little prayer of thanks.

But then again, to Whom or What was he praying?

The eight humans had blessed the candles, the wine, and the bread, while praying to something larger than themselves.

Nah. Not for him. Most things on Earth were larger than Fleabrain.

A sudden, brilliant inspiration came to him. Oh, how smart, smart, smart he was! He, Fleabrain, would pray to things *smaller* than himself! Way, way smaller than himself. Molecules. Atoms.

Sub-sub-sub-atomic somethings, singing to him from a faraway place. Because small was great.

He didn't understand it all yet. One day he would, bug it. One day, he, Fleabrain, would discover all the Truths of the Universe! He was so smart, his brain ached.

Fleabrain could hear the humans slurping their soup. Not much conversation during that part of the meal. Everyone was too hungry to discuss intellectual matters.

Now was a good time for Shoe Analysis, a pleasant little hobby of Fleabrain's. So much could be learned by studying eight pairs of shoes under a table.

Pair Number One: Professor Doctor George Gutman's.

Brand-new men's black dress shoes. Old gray socks, a tear at the ankle lovingly darned with teeny cross-stitches. Couldn't the guy afford a new pair of socks to go with the new shoes? Ah, yes. Maybe he finds it hard to replace the old socks because he misses the person who repaired them. At New Shoes' feet was a small black doctor's bag. Does a researcher make house calls? A mystery.

Pair Number Two: Nurse Olivegarten's.

Dangerously pointy, high-heeled blue sling-backs. Silk hose. Toes pointed toward the professor's.

Pair Number Three: Francine's. Oh, Francine!

Patent-leather Mary Janes, Franny's best shoes from Before, which she'd insisted on wearing instead of her ugly orthopedic ones. Nurse Olivegarten hadn't approved.

Pair Number Four: Penelope "Call me Penny!" Nelson's.

Appropriately, red penny loafers, recently spruced up with new heels. Frugal (beginning teacher's and anthropologist's salaries). Optimistic: shiny 1953 pennies tucked into the slots.

Pair Number Five: Zadie Ben's.

Brown slippers. No. Not slippers. Leather shoes with the backs worn down. Also, no shoelaces. Some things were more important than dressing like a Dapper Dan, especially when you were ninety-three years, six months, and four days old. For instance, one's comfort on short, pleasant walks. Reading books. Arriving at meals while the food was still hot. The wisest human in the room.

Pair Number Six: Saint Min's.

Clean white socks. Saddle shoes, white and black. Two coats of white shoe polish oh-so-carefully applied to the saddle shoes' white sections.

Pairs Seven and Eight, at each end of the table: Muriel's and Sammy's.

Men's new size-ten maroon wing tips with tan trim. Ladies' new size-six lime-green pumps with flawed stitching. Katzenback's Footwear's slowest-selling models of 1952, a small personal indulgence after the 1953 models came in.

Now Pumps and Wing Tips got up to bring in the rest of the meal, with the help of Saddle Shoes. Penny Loafers moved to help.

"Sit, Penny dear! Our guests are here to enjoy," said Mrs. Katzenback.

Patent-leather Mary Janes stayed still. *Oh, Francine. I know you want to help, too*, thought Fleabrain. *Everybody knows you'd help if you could.*

Dinner was served. Alf sighed with happiness as more tidbits—a lump of potato pudding, a slice of turkey, a meatball—began to rain down.

Fleabrain reveled in the conversational tidbits:

The upcoming inauguration of General Dwight D. Eisenhower and Senator Richard Nixon as president and vice president, respectively.

The country's recession and the resulting poor sales at Katzenback's Footwear.

The frightening proliferation of nuclear weapons.

Were there spies in the U.S. government? Was Joe McCarthy's Senate investigation of Communists too vicious?

"Absolutely not," said Nurse Olivegarten.

"Absolutely," said Penny.

I agree! thought Fleabrain. *A witch hunt in Congress!*

Saddle Shoes tapped with boredom.

And what about the Cold War between the U.S. and the Soviet Union?

And the Korean War between South and North Korea?

Fleabrain moaned. "Ah, humans! Such folly! So many trials and tribulations! So many wars!"

"Why worry?" Alf replied. "It's beyond anyone's control."

"Is it, Alf? Does it have to be?" asked Fleabrain.

"Don't ask me," said Alf, gulping down another meatball.

Fleabrain much preferred the sprightly conversation between Professor Doctor Gutman and Penny about the romantic style of the German composer Johannes Brahms, born May 7, 1833, died April 3, 1897.

Sling-backs tapped jealously.

"Dessert is served!" said Mr. Katzenback. "From Rosenbloom's!"

Saddle Shoes wriggled with glee. "Chocolate gems!" cried Min.

Then the table was quiet once again, to Fleabrain's great disappointment. Conversation could never compete with chocolate gems from Rosenbloom's. Fleabrain could sense Alf's anticipation, waiting for a few cake crumbs to drop.

Finally, Wing Tips stood up.

"Penny, what you see in my hand is called a *tzedakah* box," said Mr. Katzenback. "*Tzedakah* is a Hebrew word meaning 'righteous.' Every Friday evening after the Sabbath meal, my daughters do the righteous deed of placing coins from their allowance in the box. This money is collected for people less fortunate than ourselves."

"Tzeh-dack-uh. Such a beautiful little box. And what a nice tradition!" said Penny.

Saddle Shoes leaped up and ran to her father. *Clink!* went her coins into the *tzedakah* box.

Mary Janes stayed still.

"Come, Franny," said Mr. Katzenback. There was a scraping of chairs as everyone moved closer to the table in order to make room for Franny in her wheelchair.

"Oh, Dad. Just bring the box over here," said Franny.

"All right, darling. Here it is," said her father.

Clink! Clink! From her place at the table, Franny dropped her coins into the box.

Sling-backs tapped impatiently.

"If Franny had worn her braces and the proper shoes," said Nurse Olivegarten, "she could have walked the short distance to her papa. We are all thrilled that Franny has some movement in both feet and, occasionally, in her lower limbs, Doctor Gutman. I'm using Sister Kenny's methods of daily hot, wet packs and strenuous stretching. Soon our girl will be out of her wheelchair completely, just about as good as new. Show the doctor your leg movement, Franny."

Mary Janes didn't move.

Sling-backs kicked.

Mary Janes still didn't move.

Fleabrain mightily restrained himself from biting one of Sling-backs' ankles.

"Please show him, Franny!" repeated Nurse Olivegarten.

"No, I don't want to right now. But I would like to show him my wheelies," said Franny. "I do wonderful wheelies."

Min laughed. "She does!"

"I'd love to see you do wheelies," said Professor Doctor Gutman.

Mary Janes began to wheel herself from the table. Pumps stood up.

"Franny, we don't want you to tire yourself," said Mrs. Katzenback. "You need to save your strength."

"Save my strength for what? I hardly ever do *anything*," said Franny.

"Wheelies? What are wheelies?" asked Zadie Ben. It was the

first time he'd spoken during the meal. Chewing carefully, not conversing, had been the task at hand.

"Papa, wheelies mean that Franny races up and down the hallway in her wheelchair, then rears up on her wheels," said Franny's mother. "Now just isn't the time."

"This is what Franny does?" said Zadie Ben, sounding more surprised than when his family and friends had surprised him with a ninetieth birthday party, taking over almost all of Weinstein's Restaurant except a few booths at the front. "That's something I'd like to do myself," he said. "Will you teach me another day, *feygeleh*?"

Min giggled, and so did Franny, at the thought of their great-grandfather doing wheelies. Oh, how Franny loved her Zadie! She loved how he called her *feygeleh*. Little bird. He always made her feel as if she could soar, even now.

"Now is the time for schnapps in the living room for the adults, and cocoa for the girls," said Mr. Katzenback.

At that moment Not-Slippers jumped up, startling Fleabrain and Alf, whose haunches had been resting on them.

"One minute, please, folks," said Zadie Ben.

"Of course," said Mr. Katzenback. "Zadie will now say the after-dinner blessing."

Zadie Ben began to chant in Hebrew. His chanting went on and on and on, quite a bit longer than usual. Only Fleabrain seemed to notice that Zadie was no longer chanting a blessing in Hebrew but was singing a Yiddish song.

Fleabrain's heart filled with sorrow and dread.

The song was describing a Truth of the Universe.

The Yiddish words seemed to swirl around the room. They did wheelies against the walls. They broke into shards of syllables, bouncing from floor to ceiling. Fleabrain saw sparks flashing before his eyes, and his brain ached with the awful knowledge. He lay on his back, hardly breathing. He waved his limbs in distress.

"Fleabrain, my friend! What's wrong?" barked Alf.

"A bit of indigestion," Fleabrain gasped. "I'll be all right in a moment."

He would be all right, but only if he kept his knowledge a secret, especially from Francine. Knowing his dear Francine as he did, if she truly understood this particular Truth of the Universe, she wouldn't need him anymore.

Fleabrain didn't think he could bear that.

Poor Fleabrain. Poor, poor, Fleabrain, the voices sang.

How Did Our Cars Travel Without Us?

Rag

un.
night,
morrow,
high 24. We.

A2

Tuesday, January 6, 1953

TIPSY PATRONS' CARS DISAPPEAR

by Jimmy Regis, Special Correspondent

At 1:00 a.m. Sunday morning three patrons emerged from Poli's Restaurant on Murray Avenue to discover that their automobiles were nowhere to be found. An uproar ensued, alerting two Squirrel Hill police officers who happened to be patrolling the area (Murray Avenue near the Morrowfield Apartments). The officers insisted upon driving the inebriated gentlemen home, whereupon their respective cars were found parked on their respective streets.

The relieved automobile owners were certain they had driven their cars to the restaurant. "How did our cars travel without us?" asked one car owner repeatedly. The officers were seen laughing uproariously, "although driving and drinking is no laughing matter," declared Officer L. M. McFeen.

FB Saliva #2

Squawk! Squeak! Squawk!

The mystery of Professor Doctor Gutman's little black bag under the table was soon solved. It wasn't a doctor's bag but a clarinet case. The case and the clarinet inside had belonged to the professor's daughter, Sophie Harriet Gutman. Now it belonged to Francine Babette Katzenback, who had just completed a rousing rendition of "Yankee Doodle" for Fleabrain.

"Of course, I'll improve with practice," she said.

Leaping onto the arm of her wheelchair, Fleabrain clapped several claws in appreciation of her enthusiasm, if not her musical prowess.

"Professor Doctor Gutman's daughter died in Europe during the war," Franny continued, peering at Fleabrain through Sparky's Finest. "That's why his eyes are often sad. But he wants the clarinet to be played again, so he's giving me free music lessons."

Fleabrain already knew that, of course. The whole street did, too. Squeaks and squawks tooted from Franny's window even when it was closed, sounding less like music than cries for help.

Franny maneuvered her wheelchair in order to place a record on her record player, which sat on a table beside her bed. "Listen to this, Fleabrain," she said. Classical music filled the air.

"Ah," said Fleabrain. "The Mozart Concerto in A, played by the English clarinetist Jack Brymer, born January 27, 1915. There's nothing lovelier than an evening's clarinet concerto after a long day. And I must say, 'Music hath charms to soothe the savage breast,' even if that breast is only a flea's. A phrase coined by another Englishman, by the way. Writer William Congreve, born January 24, 1670, died January 19, 1729."

"The professor says I will play like that one day," said Franny. "Or almost, anyway, with years of practice."

Fleabrain hid a "smile" with his tarsi. His dear Francine had a long way to go, musically, from a squawking "Yankee Doodle" to a Mozart concerto. But he would be the last to discourage her. She looked so happy when she was squawking!

Min knocked on the door. "Franny, please lower the volume of the record player. I've got a test tomorrow."

"Oh, phoo," said Franny. But she turned off the record player. She began playing her clarinet again.

Squawk. Squeak. Squawk.

"The professor is a good teacher. I think I'm getting better," said Franny. "It's easier than my exercises with Nurse Olivegarten, and practicing the clarinet doesn't hurt."

But there was so much for her to remember! Tongue high in back at the roof of mouth. Chin flat. Lower lip over bottom teeth. Upper teeth touching top of mouthpiece, but don't bite. Tip of tongue touching tip of reed.

Tee, tee, tee. Squawk!

Min poked her head in again. "Franny! It's late. Read a book or something."

"Okeydokey, Saint," said Franny.

"Speaking of books," said Fleabrain, hopping onto the yellow afghan. "I have been thinking. Of course, I am always thinking. I think, therefore I am, and all that. But tonight I am thinking of a good book I've just completed. I practically gobbled it up."

"I know that feeling. I'm enjoying *The Black Stallion*," said Franny, pointing to the novel on her night table. "I've just finished the part about the ship sinking and the boy and the wild horse plunging into the sea. And then the boy holds on to a rope while the stallion pulls him through the raging waters, and—"

"I haven't read that book for youngsters," said Fleabrain. He waved a skinny leg dismissively. "The book I'm referring to is *Paramoigraphy*, by the English writer James Howell, born 1594, died 1666. It is his book of proverbs. I've read others by the same author. Have you perused his work, by any chance? *Paramoigraphy* is on the hallway bookshelf."

"'Perused'? Do you mean 'read'?"

"'Peruse' generally means 'to read with attention to detail,' as I certainly did, having memorized most of his work. So, yes, 'read' is what I meant."

Franny remembered the book *Paramoigraphy,* lodged between an atlas and a book called *Moby-Dick* by Herman Melville on the top shelf of the lofty bookcase. It smelled of dust and stew and had TAYLOR ALLDERDICE HIGH SCHOOL—DISCARD stamped on its inside front cover.

"I leafed through it, but the pages kept falling out," she said. Plus, it looked boring, but she didn't want to hurt Fleabrain's feelings by saying so.

"Yes, it's an oldie," said Fleabrain. "But Howell's sayings truly make me think. *He that hath eaten a bear-pie will always smell of the garden.* I love the stink of compost and hairy creatures, don't you? And *No weeping for shed milk.* Why cry, indeed? Milk is particularly delicious when putrid and smelly, a puddle on the ground."

"That *is* a different perspective," said Franny.

"The man had such literary insight! And my absolute favorite, the one that applies to you and me, my dear Francine—*All work and no play makes Jack a dull boy.* All work and no play makes Francine and Fleabrain a dull girl and dull flea."

"I don't find you dull one bit," said Franny.

"Nor I, you, Francine," said Fleabrain. "Perhaps I should rephrase. All that hosing of fires and moving of automobiles, the midwifery, the championing of truth and justice—all those good deeds have been filled with such serious purpose and moral responsibility!"

"Nothing wrong with that," said Franny. She was proud of her good deeds with Fleabrain.

Fleabrain grinned, a wiggle of his tubelike mouthparts. "Of

course there's nothing wrong with it! But, as I said, it's all work and no play. And now you have to toot on that instrument every day."

"Oh, I don't mind practicing the clarinet," said Franny. "The professor says it's good for my lungs."

Fleabrain leaped from the afghan onto the colorful braided rug by the side of the bed. "Francine, Francine, it's time for some fun!" he called up to her.

"Every single thing we've done together has been loads of fun."

Fleabrain jumped onto an arm of her wheelchair. "Francine, I'd like to try an experiment with you, if you don't mind. As you know, there are ancient spells for miniaturization," said Fleabrain, "but I think they're all hogwash."

"Miniaturization?"

"Right. The ancients, especially those of the Middle Ages, were convinced that spells could accomplish miniaturization." Fleabrain's voice tinkled with laughter. "Spells! Can you imagine? So very medieval! But I, Fleabrain, understand the science behind miniaturization. Basically, it's the manipulation of matter on an atomic and molecular scale. I've even thought of some impressive names for the science. *Nanotechnology.* Or maybe *microprocessing.* Which do you think sounds more impressive?"

"Both sound very impressive," said Franny. "But why are you interested in miniaturization? You're so small, I can only see you with Sparky's Finest."

Fleabrain's giggles were tiny peeps. "Oh, Francine, I wasn't talking about myself. It was you to whom I was referring!"

"Me? Miniaturized?" said Franny a little apprehensively.

"As a researcher, I really should ask your permission to minia-turize you. Do I have it? I hope you say yes!"

"Will it hurt?" Franny asked.

"You will feel odd, but it won't hurt, I promise. Was Alice in *Alice's Adventures in Wonderland* in pain? Not at all. Admittedly, Alice was fictional, but I believe her creator, the English writer Lewis Carroll, born Charles L. Dodgson, born January 27, 1832, died January 14, 1898, was a terrific visionary in terms of miniaturization. Hopefully, I've perfected the process. No chewing of Eat Me tablets or mushrooms necessary."

"Permission granted. Proceed," said Franny. She realized that she trusted Fleabrain with all her heart.

"Hold out an index finger, if you please."

When Franny did so, Fleabrain daintily squirted liquid from his mouthparts onto the tip of her finger. "Let's try some FB Saliva #2. Simply dab this behind your ears and at your wrists, as you would a sweet *eau de toilette*. Sorry. That's French for 'toilet water' or 'cologne.'"

Franny dabbed. FB Saliva #2 smelled odd but familiar, not sweet at all.

"Close your eyes, take a few nice deep breaths, and relax," Fleabrain said.

Franny squeezed her eyes shut. She heard a *pfffft!* sound, like a fuse blowing, or a balloon losing its air. The room suddenly smelled of popcorn and firecrackers, a pleasant, partylike odor. Her scalp tingled. Her head bobbed, and her hands waved. She felt an odd squeezing sensation on her skin, similar to the tight feeling she always got after a summer sunburn.

She had been through worse. Much worse. There was no pain to miniaturization at all, just as Fleabrain had promised. It was a very strange experience but nothing she couldn't get used to.

"Francine," Fleabrain whispered, his voice trembling with love and awe. "You can open your eyes now."

Miniaturized

It was a new world, and it took Franny's breath away.

At first she saw only a bright kaleidoscope of undulating objects. Huge brown trees, even bigger than prehistoric redwoods, with deeply engrained black rivulets. A rainbow of small mountain ranges. A large swath of heavenly sunshine, high above her head.

Franny felt dizzy, swaying a bit in her wheelchair.

"Breathe, Francine, breathe," said Fleabrain. "Don't try to understand the very big. Focus on what is relative to your new size, one thing at a time. It will make the adjustment easier."

Fleabrain's voice was no longer squeaky. It was a wise, deep voice with vibrato around its edges, like the strumming of a guitar.

Franny did as he told her. She focused on a dust particle, which looked like a tumbleweed floating by. She stared up at a swooping, splendid highway of moonlight. She stared down at a crumb, which looked as big as a hunk of bread by the wheel of her chair. Her wheelchair had been miniaturized, too, as had everything Franny had been touching during the miniaturization procedure. That included Sparky's Finest. Since Franny no longer needed it for magnification purposes, she dropped it into the pocket of her blouse for safekeeping.

Sophie Harriet Gutman's former clarinet was now smaller than an eyelash, a mere splinter of what it used to be. Franny felt guilty that the precious family heirloom had been accidentally miniaturized. But the guilty feeling was only momentary. Of course the process could be reversed! Besides, Franny was much too excited to worry about the larger world at that moment.

For there she was, miraculously face-to-"face" with Fleabrain, who was perched proudly on top of a green hill. How handsome he was! His tubelike mouthparts; his tiny, expressive eyes; the neatly combed hairs on his body. And his legs! What wonders! Six of them, the hind legs formidably long for leaping. Now Franny could easily see each distinctive leg part: the coxa, the femur, the graceful tibia, the balletic tarsus, the claw. Of course, Fleabrain was just as handsome as ever, but up close he was so much more complex, so interesting, so *regal*. He reminded Franny of the drawing of a great Egyptian pharaoh in her history book, *Worlds Far Away and Long Ago*. He smelled strongly of earth and Alf and, yes, blood, but it was a familiar, soothing odor. And exactly the smell of FB Saliva #2 *eau de toilette*.

She breathed deeply. Soon the kaleidoscope stopped undulating and began to make sense. The giant brown trees were the legs of her matching bedroom set—her desk, her chair, her bed. The deep black rivulets were the scratches on them. The rainbow mountain ranges were the braids of the rug, and the swath of heavenly sunshine, her afghan, draped on the bed above her.

"Laissez les bon temps rouler!" said Fleabrain. "Translation: 'Let the good times roll!'"

One's eyes were supposed to be mirrors to the soul. Although Fleabrain's were teeny-tiny and on either side of his head, they did seem to be twinkling with merriment. His whole body was quivering with excitement.

"What good times?" asked Franny.

"Of course you've heard of flea circuses?"

"I've read about them," said Franny. "But I always thought they were imaginary."

Fleabrain "smiled," a sad, rueful smile. "Ah, no, my dear Francine. They were as real as can be, and tantamount to severe and cruel abuse. Circus fleas have suffered greatly, believe you me."

"I do know about the abuse of other circus creatures," said Franny. "Bears on chains, forced to dance and ride tricycles, majestic lions cooped up in cages, monkeys wearing silly costumes!"

"Indeed," said Fleabrain. "My own kind also wore silly costumes, and tight chains of silk thread around their 'necks.' They were deliberately frightened by loud noises so that they'd jump involuntarily, thus appearing to pull huge carts and battleships and coaches. 'Huge' in a relative sense, of course, but still heartbreaking. They were humiliated and overworked for fun and profit by cruel humans."

"That *is* terrible," agreed Franny. "I'm so sorry."

Fleabrain leaped an inch. "But that was then, and this is now! I've still got enough of the kid in me to love the circus, as long as the participants can control the show in a humane way. So now, to the tune of 'Entrance of the Gladiators,' by the Czech composer Julius Fučík, born July 18, 1872, died September 15, 1916, we present F and F's Fantastic Circus!"

And it began.

Fleabrain the Ringmaster waved a few tibiae, thrillingly whistling the familiar circus theme song Franny had heard a zillion times.

Scores of silverfish playfully emerged from an electrical outlet, then cavorted on the circus-ring rug in perfect musical time.

Fleabrain the Tumbler backflipped and high-jumped his way over to the silverfish. Whistling, he tapped his tarsi in a performance that put famous dancer Gene Kelly to shame.

A cockroach rode a nickel like a unicycle all around the room.

Multicolored particles bounced to the ceiling, artfully juggled by talented dust mites.

"Prepare to be amazed!" hollered Fleabrain. "Behold, the Amazing Alf!"

A thunderous earthquake shook the circus ring.

The Amazing Alf had rolled over.

"And there's more! Here she is, the Fantastic Francine!"

The Fantastic Francine lifted iron nails many times her weight, her arms strong and muscular from pushing the wheels of her chair.

The Fantastic Francine was shot through a cannon/straw, landing in Fleabrain's "arms."

"And now, the Fantastic Francine will perform a high-wire feat never before performed in a wheelchair, big *or* small!" cried Fleabrain, helping Franny into her chair again.

He lifted Franny and her wheelchair above his head, then leaped to an impossible height, even for a flea. A previously unnoticed cobweb hung in a corner of the ceiling. Carefully, Fleabrain deposited Franny on a web strand, then jumped to another strand to watch her performance.

Franny's strong arms, her wheelie practice, and her intimate knowledge of wheelchair dynamics allowed her to scoot and swerve expertly from sticky strand to sticky strand, correctly positioning the wheels to accomplish the maneuvers.

Wriggling his limbs in delight, even Fleabrain seemed surprised by the feats of the Fantastic Francine! Franny herself was exhilarated but not surprised. She'd had a feeling she could do it, although she was surprised at what a wonderful time she was having. She swooped and turned and balanced and wheeled, a small wind blowing at her back. It was almost as much fun as flying over Pittsburgh on Lightning.

But then . . .

Franny heard the creature before she saw him. His cry was like the keening of a cat and the hiss of a snake, an unearthly combination. Looking up, Franny saw the huge brown spider squeezing out of a crack in the wall. His several pairs of eyes focused on Franny and Fleabrain with a ravenous fury.

"I've got him within my sights," whispered Fleabrain. "He has no idea whom he's up against."

The spider's long legs advanced surely and confidently toward his prey, toward the seemingly helpless flea and the creature of flesh in the wheeled contraption. The web trembled as the spider reached their strands.

"Never fear, Francine!" cried Fleabrain.

Franny *was* afraid of the advancing spider, but she also felt sorry for him. He was at an unfair advantage because of Fleabrain's unnatural superpowers, as well as Fleabrain's anti-spider bias. The spider, on the other hand, about to paralyze his prey, was just doing what came naturally. Not to mention the fact that his web had become a playground for a disrespectful circus troupe.

"Watch me pulverize him," sneered Fleabrain. "Watch me chew him to bloody smithereens. No. Watch me extract each leg, each eye, each hair, slowly and painstakingly, until he screams for mercy. *Then* watch me pulverize him!"

Franny was saddened to see that Fleabrain, once such a rational and compassionate creature, had become a vicious warmonger.

She rocked her wheelchair with sudden force, breaking several web strands. Falling through a gaping hole, she propelled herself downward, aiming her wheelchair carefully. The chair's speed accelerated as it neared its destination, finally splashing down into the water tray under the "Cheer up!" dracaena plant.

"Alf, come!" Franny called. Grateful to have passed her Level 3 Junior Red Cross swim test before she got polio, she swam a speedy Australian crawl through the current, using only her upper body. A short distance from the edge, she grabbed Alf's tail and was pulled from the water tray.

"Lie down, Alf," said Franny.

Far above her, the combatants were at a silent standoff, motionless before the attack.

Franny dragged herself to the tip of Alf's tail, then reached down to grab her clarinet from the rug.

Tongue high in back at the roof of mouth. Chin flat. Lower lip over bottom teeth. Upper teeth touching top of mouthpiece, but don't bite. Tip of tongue touching tip of reed. Franny blew a G note with all her might.

It was a small sound, but it was glorious—strong and steady, neither a squeak nor a squawk. The beautiful little note filled the room, all the way up to the ceiling. Was it enough to "soothe the savage breasts," the spider's and the flea's?

It was.

Several seconds later, Fleabrain joined her on the rug. The glorious little G note still hung in the air, like a lovely *eau de toilette*.

"Thank you. We needed that," Fleabrain said. "I don't know what came over me, although I think I understand what was irking the spider. But how satisfying to see the spider's surprise when my superstrength allowed me to escape his sticky bonds!"

Fleabrain retrieved the wheelchair, which was floating in the water tray like a paddleboat. He dried it off with a piece of lint, then helped Franny slide from Alf into the chair.

"Fleabrain, I'd like to be my regular size again, please," said Franny.

"Oh," said Fleabrain. "Of course."

Franny heard a trace of disappointment in his voice.

"It's just that I want to play the beautiful note for my family," she explained.

Franny felt exhilarated! She was now hopeful that with practice she would progress beyond the patriotic but boring "Yankee Doodle." She was like little Rose Goodly, who was just learning to read

143

those baby books about Dick and Jane. Rose complained that Dick and Jane were boring, boring, boring. *You have to start at the beginning*, everyone told her. Although Dick and Jane *were* boring, always hollering, "Oh, oh, oh!" at ordinary things—for example, their dog, Spot, running away from a frog. If they were miniaturized, Dick and Jane would probably drop dead from excitement.

But practice makes perfect. Practice would make her walk, too.

"I hope you enjoyed yourself in my world," Fleabrain said anxiously.

"Oh, yes! I had an interesting, exciting time," said Franny.

"I'm so glad. Hold on while I begin the maximizing process with some FB Saliva Negative #2. Kindly give me your monocle, if you please."

Franny handed him the miniaturized Sparky's Finest, and Fleabrain squirted fluid onto its lens. "Close your eyes now," he said, clasping the anointed bottle cap and focusing it on Franny. "Prepare to return to your natural size. It will be a slow but steady process."

Franny closed her eyes, holding her clarinet tightly. There was that smell of firecrackers and popcorn again.

"We'll be friends forever, won't we?" she heard Fleabrain ask as he carefully returned Sparky's Finest to the pocket of her blouse.

"Of course we will," Franny answered, already feeling herself growing larger. It was a feeling that reminded her of happiness.

Poster Child

Franny's mother shook the newspaper at the breakfast table.

"Listen to this," she said. "'If you lined up a bunch of dimes, you would need exactly 92,160 of them to make a mile. That's $9,216.' Whoever figured that out has a lot of time on their hands! 'This week, mothers in Pittsburgh will be collecting money for the March of Dimes, trying to amass a Mile of Dimes like other cities in the U.S.' Well, I believe I'm going to be one of those marchers."

The March of Dimes was like a great big *tzedakah* box—an organization collecting dimes for the unfortunate victims of polio and for polio research. Franny used to think of the "unfortunate" as people who were hungry or cold and very poor, like the boy in her song with blistered feet who had to wear his sister's clothes. Sometimes she'd see photographs of those unfortunates in the newspaper: children with huge eyes, wrapped in dingy blankets and holding empty bowls. Or photographs of unshaven older men eating a holiday dinner at a long table in a church hall.

But, of course, polio victims were unfortunates, too. There were posters of the March of Dimes poster children everywhere, it seemed—in libraries, stores, and banks. There was a photograph of one of them in that day's newspaper.

When Franny looked at the top half of the poster child, ignoring the bottom half showing the little boy's braces and wheelchair, he was a regular kid, laughing with joy. A kindly nurse laid a gentle hand on his shoulder. There were other children in the photo, children who didn't have polio, crowding around the poster child's wheelchair like really good buddies.

She herself would make a terrible poster child. And the only good buddy in *her* newspaper photo would be Fleabrain, who would look like a speck of dust on the page. No, not even a speck of dust. You wouldn't even see him at all.

Fleabrain. Dear, dear Fleabrain.

As if reading Franny's mind, Min said, "If you were a poster child, you'd stick out your tongue at the camera. Or bury your head in a book, foaming at the mouth."

That made Franny laugh, because it was sort of true. Sometimes only a sister was allowed to say something sort of true, and then it became funny.

"Or I'd play 'Yankee Doodle' over and over on my clarinet until the photographer ran away screaming," said Franny.

Fleabrain himself had put forth his opinion about all of this.

"Francine, those happy poster children are part of a giant marketing campaign to collect funds! Don't get me started on modern advertising! It's too unpleasant for people to open their newspaper and see a crabby poster child. That, my dear, would be an oxymoron, like a giant shrimp. Or a wise fool."

Now Franny's father glanced at the poster child's photo. "A photo should encourage people to donate money, and this one is doing its job. The newspapers and the March of Dimes are educating the public about polio, as well as saving the Katzenbacks from debtors' prison." Mr. Katzenback smiled a little when he said that, so Franny wasn't really worried about her parents going to jail for their debts. Still, she was glad that some of the medical bills for her care were being paid by the March of Dimes.

And those bills included Nurse Olivegarten's.

"I fear this child isn't cooperating. Her muscles aren't loosening as fast as I'd like," Nurse Olivegarten said at Franny's exercise session that day.

"Franny, you do need to practice your standing and walking more often," said her mother. "Nurse Olivegarten is working hard on you, for your own good."

"In my opinion, Muriel, she needs to buck up and cultivate a more pleasant, can-do attitude," said Nurse Olivegarten.

Who was Nurse Olivegarten to talk about being pleasant? thought Franny, lying on the kitchen table. When Nurse Olivegarten "worked on" Franny, she never looked Franny in the eye. She always had a mustache of sweat on her upper lip and a frown on her forehead. Nurse Olivegarten made Franny feel like a broken-down car in an automotive repair shop, or a chicken about to be plucked.

"We got movement before, and we'll get it again. Believe you me,

I know what I'm talking about," said Nurse Olivegarten. "I need you to cooperate with me and practice your walking more often."

"Believe you me," Franny said, "I want me to walk just as much as you do."

Once Franny was off the list of unfortunates, Nurse Olivegarten wouldn't have to come anymore. It was worrisome that Nurse Olivegarten had started calling her parents Muriel and Sammy, like a member of the family who would be around forever.

And, Franny thought, *I am a practicer and a cooperator! Ask Professor Doctor George Gutman! Ask me to play any one of three, almost four, songs on my clarinet!*

"This girl has a beautiful *embouchure*," Professor Doctor Gutman had told her parents. "She has been working hard in bringing her teeth and lips and tongue into excellent alignment with the mouthpiece. No easy feat, I tell you."

Franny was proud of her *embouchure.* She wished her legs would be as cooperative after practice as her teeth and lips and tongue were.

But Nurse Olivegarten and Min were right about one thing. She wasn't a bucker-upper about her condition. It would be hard for her to pretend to be joyful, even for a camera. It wasn't only the polio anymore, really. Sometimes Franny felt like a girl from another planet, lost in the mysteries of outer space. Even if that girl could move all her limbs while she floated around up there, it wouldn't make a bit of difference if she felt alone in the dark.

Thank goodness for Fleabrain. Dear, dear Fleabrain!

On Wednesday evening, almost every porch light on Shady

Avenue was bright, a signal to the Mothers' March that dimes could be collected at those homes. Aunt Pauline telephoned to borrow a bulb.

"No marchers have reached our block yet. I'll bring a lightbulb right over," Franny's mother said. "Then let's march together."

Franny watched with Min from the living room window. Their mother scurried across the street, wearing her heavy duffel coat against the bitter cold.

Soon a group of Mothers' Marchers rounded the corner. Franny's mother and Aunt Pauline joined them. The marchers were singing like Christmas carolers, but they were singing the same exuberant tune, over and over. The tune was that of a song from Franny's favorite movie, *Snow White and the Seven Dwarfs*. "Heigh-ho, heigh-ho! It's off to work we go!" sang the dwarfs. The marchers' words were different.

"Heigh-ho! Heigh-ho! We'll fight that polio! Heigh-ho! Heigh-ho! We'll fight that polio!" they sang.

The honks of car horns greeting the marchers became a happy accompaniment to their song. The marchers swarmed down the street, ringing doorbells, waving at their Squirrel Hill neighbors. Fathers marched, and children, too, who were excited to be outside after dark. They ran beside their parents like trick-or-treaters, wearing heavy snowsuits instead of costumes.

"Heigh-ho! Heigh-ho! We'll fight that polio! Heigh-ho! Heigh-ho! We'll fight that polio!"

Franny's father opened their front door, with Franny in her

wheelchair, and Min behind him. He gave one of the marchers several special March of Dimes cardboard booklets, their slots filled up with dimes. Franny peeked from behind his legs.

There was Teresa and Rose Goodly, and the A through C Solomon siblings. Other kids she knew were calling her name from across the street. Franny searched for Walter Walter in the small crowd but couldn't find him.

Someone yelled, "It's Franny Katzenback!" Others joined in: "Franny! Hey, Franny! Franny!"

People began to clap, their gloves and mittens making muted thumps. They were clapping for her—Franny! Franny looked up at her father and saw tears in his eyes. She stretched her mouth into a big smile. She didn't want her father to cry. Franny understood a little better then how a poster child must feel, relieved to know that others understood the difficulty of it all. She was grateful to the newspapers and the March of Dimes for educating the public. But they were clapping for her as if she'd *done* something. All she'd done was get polio.

"We miss you, Franny," called Teresa.

But which Franny? Franny wanted to ask. *Which Franny do you miss? Because, actually, I've been here all along. In the flesh.*

The crowd, including Teresa and the others, moved on down the street, singing, "Heigh-ho! Heigh-ho! We'll fight that polio!" into the cold night air.

Only Quiet Katy Green and her parents remained on the doorstep.

"So! This is Franny," said Quiet Katy's dad. He was wearing

a TONIGHT I AM A MOTHER sign pinned to his jacket. "Katy talks about you all the time."

Quiet Katy's cheeks, already pink from the cold, grew pinker. "Oh, Daddy," she whispered.

"Oops, my big mouth again. I'm the loudmouth in the family," he said. "Katy and Sally are the shy ones. Two peas in a pod."

"Oh, Carl," said Quiet Katy's mother, Sally. She put an arm around her daughter and smiled. Quiet Katy and her mother did look very much alike, with their round cheeks and watchful eyes.

"Come inside to warm up for a bit," said Mr. Katzenback.

Before Franny knew it, the adults were sitting down for tea, Min had excused herself, and Franny and Quiet Katy were alone in Franny's bedroom. Alf followed them in.

Quiet Katy looked around. "What a nice room!" she said. "I love your braided rug. I've got the same ballerina alarm clock! And you play the clarinet. I'm taking music lessons, too! My parents said I could choose any instrument, any instrument at all. I chose the trombone! Oh, you've got a dog! Lucky, lucky you! My parents won't let me get one because my father has allergies, even though he's allergic to cats, but he doesn't want to take a chance, in case he's allergic to dogs, too, and then it would be too late, because we'd all love that dog and wouldn't want to return it. Let me see your books. Oh, I've read a lot of them! Didn't you love *Little House in the Big Woods* and *The Secret Garden*? Wasn't *Little Women* wonderful? I thought I'd read the entire Bobbsey Twins series, but you have some I haven't even read yet!"

Franny realized Quiet Katy wasn't actually that shy or quiet.

"Oh, what's this?" cried Quiet Katy, or just plain Katy at that moment. She held up Sparky's Finest. "Is this a brooch? It's really nice."

"It's a bottle cap," said Franny. "One of my favorites."

"It's unusual for a bottle cap." Katy waved Sparky's Finest around the room. "Look how it catches the light!"

Franny caught a quick flash of Fleabrain's "face," on Alf's tail, looking alarmed. Franny was alarmed, as well. "Careful, please. Don't drop it."

"Oh, of course," said Katy respectfully. She gently laid Sparky's Finest on Franny's dresser again.

"I could lend you some Bobbsey Twins books, the ones you haven't read," said Franny. "And any other books you want to borrow."

"Oh, good! Thank you!" Katy chose a few books from the bookshelf. "I'll take really, really good care of these; don't you worry. I'm not the type who folds down the corners of her pages, so you don't have to worry about that. Sometimes I do snack while I read, but I promise I won't do that, either. But if I do snack, I'll make sure I'm really, really careful. I'll use lots of napkins. I'll shake out any crumbs. And if I do any permanent damage, I promise I'll replace your book. But, as I said, don't worry. I'll be really careful."

Katy stopped to take a breath. "Franny, I'm really, really glad we got a chance to spend time in a one-to-one situation. I always feel much better in a one-to-one situation. Shyness is an affliction of mine and my mother's. Oh, I guess I shouldn't say 'affliction.' I'm really sorry. I didn't mean—"

"I'm glad we got a chance to spend time, too," said Franny.

Franny wheeled over to her bedside, because there was one more book to lend Katy, the one she always kept on her night table. "Here's something else for you," she said. "My very favorite."

Katy examined the cover. "A book about a spider and a pig?"

"It's recently published," said Franny. "You'll love it."

Proud Pittsburgh

Friday, January 30, 1953

MOTHERS' MARCH BOOSTS POLIO FUND TO $186,000 AND STILL COUNTING!

The Mothers' March to raise funds for fighting polio went over the top Wednesday night, in spite of the severe weather. Organizers expect still more dimes to come in from several other communities.

"Heigh-ho," indeed! That's over twenty miles of dimes! A proud moment in our history, Pittsburgh!

Dr. Engel, Who Thought He Knew Everything

Franny knew the face of her pediatrician, Dr. Harris Engel, very well. She'd spent time with it, up close, during every examination, all her life. Dr. Engel's breath smelled like peppermint and cigars. He had two deep lines in his broad forehead, lines that seemed deeper every time Franny saw him. As he loomed over her, Franny could even count the nose hairs growing from Dr. Engel's nostrils. His cheeks were chubby and tanned, even though it was February. That's because Dr. and Mrs. Engel had recently returned from Florida.

"Say 'ah,'" said Dr. Engel, holding down Franny's tongue with a wooden stick.

"Ah," said Franny. She counted the nose hairs. Three hairs this visit—two hanging from the left nostril and one from the right.

"Throat looks normal," he said. "Now for your ears." He leaned over and poked Franny's ears with his ear-examining contraption.

"Did you have a nice vacation, Doctor?" asked Mrs. Katzenback.

"Mmm," said Dr. Engel.

"That's nice," said Franny's mother, although to Franny it wasn't clear whether Dr. Engel meant yes or no.

Dr. Engel never seemed to like talking about personal matters. She actually knew very little about him, except that there was a Mrs. Engel and they went to Florida the first two weeks of every single February. It was hard to imagine Dr. Engel lying on a beach in bathing trunks, baring his large stomach. Franny had never seen him in anything except his white coat and crisply pressed long pants.

"We wanted to make an earlier appointment, but your nurse reminded us that you were vacationing," said Mr. Katzenback.

"Turn this way, dear." Dr. Engel poked Franny's other ear. "Was there an urgent need? You certainly could have made an appointment with Dr. Unger while I was gone."

"No, it wasn't urgent," said Mr. Katzenback. "We were, as I believe I told your nurse, worried about Franny's lack of greater progress in terms of moving her legs."

"Oh, but she *has* made progress!" said Franny's mother. "We are thrilled that she has moved her feet since we last saw you! And she does walk short distances with her braces, even without the crutches. Show the doctor, Franny."

Her father eased Franny out of her wheelchair, helping her stand upright. Franny leaned hard on one braced leg, then pushed her opposite hip forward so that her other braced leg swung out stiffly. She reversed the process with the other leg, clinging to her father's arm, continuing to walk this way to the doctor's big desk, then back again to her chair, into which she sank with relief.

"We are wondering if you would write a note to the authorities at Creswell School, describing her progress with her braces and crutches, and allaying any fears they might have of contagion," said Mr. Katzenback.

"Of course, of course," said Dr. Engel, adding to the notes on his clipboard.

"But she will improve even more and walk normally again, won't she, Doctor?" asked Franny's father.

"Mmm," said Dr. Engel.

"We also have some concerns about her eyes," said Mrs. Katzenback.

"Her eyes?" asked the doctor.

Franny squirmed in her wheelchair. "Oh, Mom. I told you. I was just pretending."

"That may be, but we thought a quick eye exam would set our fears to rest. Franny has been fitting a glass bottle cap inside her eyeglasses to correct her vision, Doctor."

"I wasn't *correcting* anything," Franny said. "I just wanted to pretend I was wearing a monocle, like people used to do in olden times."

"Honey, it seems you've pretended more than once. All of us have noticed you wearing the bottle cap several times in the past few weeks," said her mother.

"Just a quick exam, Doctor," said Mr. Katzenback, "as long as we're here. And, if necessary, we'll take her to her ophthalmologist for a stronger eyeglass prescription."

Still wearing her glasses, Franny rattled off the letters on the eye chart, first covering her right eye and then her left, starting with the giant *E* and proceeding all the way down to the almost-invisibles. "E, F, P, T, O, Z, L, P, E, D, P, E, C, F, D, E, D . . ."

"Excellent," said Dr. Engel. "Her vision with her current prescription seems fine, Sam."

"See? I told you," said Franny.

"I just don't understand—"

Dr. Engel interrupted Mrs. Katzenback. He turned his back on Franny and put an arm on one shoulder of each of her parents. "Muriel. Sam," he said in a low voice. Dr. Engel paused, then gave a deep sigh. "I don't have to tell you what your daughter has endured. Is *still* enduring. I don't have to tell you how her life has changed and that she is extremely lonely. Surely you understand how an active imagination can add a little pleasure to her life."

"Of course we do, Doctor," said Franny's father.

Franny's eyes smarted with tears.

You were not supposed to punch a doctor in the nose. Actually, you were not supposed to punch *anyone* in the nose if you were brought up to be a good citizen, except maybe in certain situations. The only times Franny had seen noses punched were in cartoons and movies. But if she had the nerve, which she didn't, and if she could reach his nose from her wheelchair, which she couldn't, this was certainly a real-life nose-punching situation.

How dare he talk about her as if she weren't there, as if she were a strange, unlikeable girl just because she'd gotten polio! As if there was no hope that things would ever get better; as if she didn't have, *couldn't have*, a good friend or two! And as if Dr. Harris Engel knew every single thing there was to know, and Muriel and Sam were dumb (and why weren't they Mr. and Mrs. Katzenback to *him*?), just because they worried about their daughter.

Dr. Engel turned and bent over Franny in her chair, speaking to her in a loud voice as if not only her legs but her ears weren't working properly. "All right, young lady! It's been so good to see you again! Just continue the exercises with your caregiver!"

"I will, Harry," said Franny.

And then, courtesy of her active imagination, Dr. Engel stood before her in floral bathing trunks, a yellow-ducky tube around his belly because he'd never learned to swim.

Doctors didn't know everything.

Horsey! Horsey!

Wednesday, February 18, 1953

KIDS SAVED FROM EATING RAT POISON!

by Jimmy Regis, Special Correspondent

A dog's loud barking at the dining room window of a home on Northumberland Street saved the lives of two very lucky tykes. Mr. and Mrs. John Blackwelder, sipping tea after supper, were alerted to their children's near-attempt to eat poisonous, strychnine-filled pellets used to kill rats, which the kids had found under the kitchen sink.

"It looked like caramel popcorn," said Johnny Junior, age five. "Popcorn," repeated little Heather Ann, age two.

"How foolish of us to keep those pellets under the sink within the children's reach!" cried Mrs. Blackwelder.

A relieved Mr. Blackwelder said, "That dog just kept howling, racing back and forth from the dining room window to the back kitchen door."

"Looked like a wolf to me," said Mrs. Blackwelder.

"But, then again, little Heather Ann ran to the window, shouting 'Horsey! Horsey!'" interjected Mr. Blackwelder.

The couple stated that the dog or wolf or horse seemed to disappear into thin air as soon as they removed their children from danger.

Happy Birthday to Franny

Franny mailed out six invitations to her eleventh-birthday celebration, to be held Sunday afternoon, March 1, 2:00 P.M., with cake and ice cream. Walter Walter noted in one of his Get Well cards that he couldn't make it. The mother of the A, B, and C Solomon siblings phoned with her sincerest regrets, as the family would be traveling to Highland Park that day.

On the morning of the party, the dining room table was set for three with good china and flatware, a pink-and-yellow-striped tablecloth, and a two-layer cake from the Waldorf Bakery, dark chocolate icing with lacy pink birthday wishes. Alf lay by Franny's wheelchair as she waited for the guests to arrive. At 1:45 P.M., Teresa Goodly phoned to say she had to visit her great-aunt, but she'd probably stop by to drop off her gift in the late afternoon. Franny's mother removed a place setting and moved the two other settings closer together.

"I hope Katy comes," said Franny.

"Of course she will," said Mrs. Katzenback. "And we'll have another celebration with the family tonight."

Franny was wearing her favorite dress, golden yellow with punctuation marks all over it—commas and semicolons and exclamation and question marks. And her Mary Janes. "There will be lots of leftover cake!" she said, trying to joke, her voice trembling with disappointment.

Oh, pooh, why care? thought Fleabrain. Birthday parties were a needless, pagan ritual, originally observed by the ancients at a time when birthday horoscopes and birthday omens were used to forecast droughts and cattle disease.

And then there was the infamous Roman Emperor Caligula, born August 31, AD 12, died January 24, AD 41, who considered himself a god. He organized a lavish birthday party for his baby daughter, which included two days of horse racing and the ritual slaughter of three hundred bears and five hundred assorted other beasts.

Such disgusting excess! thought Fleabrain, *not to mention all those homeless fleas as a result of the slaughter.* He lay very still at the tip of Alf's tail, made sick to his stomach by this knowledge.

Still, he was happy for Francine when Katy arrived at five minutes past two. And he had to admit that the modern tradition of birthday cake and gifts was a big improvement over grim omens and dead animals.

"Would you like some hot chocolate?" Franny asked her guest. "With a marshmallow on top?"

"Don't mind if I do," said Katy, offering her cup. "Franny, I'm so glad this is a one-to-one party. Because of, you know, my—"

"Affliction!" said Franny.

"Right," said Katy.

Both girls giggled.

"Teresa is going to drop by. Maybe," said Franny.

"It's a really, really lovely party, just the way it is," said Katy.

Fleabrain thought it was a devastatingly boring birthday party. Not that he'd ever attended another, but any fool would come to the same conclusion. Sprightly conversation was vital at social gatherings! The devastatingly boring conversation at *this* party revolved around *Charlotte's Web*, both girls' favorite book (Katy had her own copy now), as well as the unremarkable coincidences in that both girls' names ended in *y* and their favorite color was yellow. Not one smidgen of a mention of current events or Nietzsche or Shakespeare or even Howell's *Paramoigraphy*! And the music, if you could call it that! Was any tune more devastatingly boring than "Happy Birthday to You"? Especially when tooted on the clarinet?

After playing the song, Franny leaned over her beautiful, fancy cake and blew out the candles. Katy clapped.

"The birthday person isn't supposed to provide her own music, but 'Happy Birthday' is such a nice, easy song, I couldn't resist," Franny said.

"When you come to my house, bring your clarinet, and we'll do a duet. I can play that song on the trombone."

Franny frowned. "Doesn't your house have a long staircase in front?"

"Yes, it does," said Katy. "But that shouldn't be a problem. We'll make a friendship seat for you. You know the kind I mean."

Katy held her left wrist with her right hand.

"Oh, I see," said Franny, doing the same.

Then the girls clasped one another's wrists with their free hands to make a "seat."

"See?" said Katy. "My mom or dad will be at one end, and I'll be at the other. And you'll be sitting in this seat as we carry you up the stairs."

"A friendship seat," said Franny.

"Stronger than rope," said Katy. The girls swung their linked arms together.

"Now, time for cake!" Franny said.

"Oh, please open my gift first," said Katy. "I can't wait for you to see it."

Franny took several moments to carefully untie the yellow ribbon and open the brightly wrapped small package. The gift was a crocheted yellow spiderweb.

An utterly useless and ridiculous gift! thought Fleabrain. *Poor Francine.*

"I'm learning to crochet. Spiderwebs are really, really easy to make, because if you make a mistake, it hardly shows," Katy said. "You can use it as a coaster for a glass of water on your night table, or hang it on the wall for decoration, or use it as a hanky."

Oh, for goodness' sake, thought Fleabrain. *How can you blow your nose if your hanky has holes in it?*

"It's beautiful," said Franny. "It could also be used as a table protector under a potted plant. Or a bookmark for *Charlotte's Web!*"

"What a really, really wonderful idea," said Katy.

You both must be joking, thought Fleabrain.

But now he was worried.

As he matured day by day, he was absorbing the Truths of the Universe at a rapid pace. Aside from the Truth he'd learned from Great-grandfather Zadie Ben (a truth he couldn't even bear to think about), there were many other truths he was acquiring, truths he supposed everyone learned as they went through life, including:

The day is long when you are bored but whizzes by when you are having fun.

The night is long when you are awake and as nervous as a cockroach but whizzes by when you're asleep.

Odors—perfume, excrement, garlic—call up memories, and everyone's memories are unique.

No two dog hairs are exactly the same.

Several good friends are nice to have, but one good friend is enough to make you happy. Sometimes one is all you need, really.

That was the worrisome truth.

"Thank you, Katy. It's the best birthday gift ever," Franny said.

We'll see about that, thought Fleabrain. *We'll just see about that!*

FB Saliva #1-X

His dear Francine deserved much more than a table protector for a potted plant. With holes, no less.

Fleabrain knew the perfect birthday gift, inspired by an old coloring book of Franny's. Although she had long since outgrown crayoning in coloring books, Franny had kept this one for its fascinating content. It was called *Let's Visit the Seven Wonders of the World!* Mrs. Nelson, aware of Franny's interest, had brought her several books about the Wonders. After reading them, Franny had carefully outlined each Wonder in the coloring book with a Crayola Black crayon, lightly shading in the rest with hues she hoped were true.

Fleabrain planned to show Francine the true colors of the Seven Wonders, one Wonder on each of seven nights. A birthday week of Wonders! An around-the-world extravaganza, a lollapalooza tour of Wonders!

The gift would require an application of FB Saliva #1-X for speed-of-light warp drive, woof and whinny travel.

"A drop on each hoof, paw, and ear will allow us to travel in a flash," Fleabrain told Franny. "I promise, there will be no jet lag the following day. Just wonderful memories."

"Oh, Fleabrain!" Franny opened the coloring book to its Table of Contents. "Stonehenge. The Leaning Tower of Pisa. The Colosseum. The Catacombs of Kom el Shoqafa. The Hagia Sophia. The Taj Mahal. The Great Wall of China. Do we have to go in order?"

Fleabrain smiled. "My dear Francine, there is no order, except that which you yourself create."

A Wondrous Travel Journal

WONDER #1
STONEHENGE

FK:

Leaving at 3:00 A.M., we zoomed instantly east across the Atlantic in order to arrive in Salisbury, England, at eight in the morning. Several tourists were already there. I pretended I was a local who was riding her horse and exercising her dog. My imitation of Queen Elizabeth's accent helped.

Stonehenge is beautiful and mysterious, just as I knew it would be. My coloring book had posed many questions: Who built it? Why? When? How did they move those heavy stones? Experts, as well as FB, have some probable theories, below.

I have used a mixture of Silver, Gray, and Prussian Blue crayons in my coloring book, but they don't truly capture what's in my mind.

FB:

A magnificent wonder!

Yet

one has to chuckle! The medievals thought the Wizard Merlin had built it!

A bit of excavating in the area on my part easily revealed pieces of decorated, flat-based pottery. Thus, Stonehenge was built around 2500 BC, during the Neolithic period.

And how were those heavy stones moved?

I put forth this theory: Could there be an ancestral connection from that era?

A Neolithic Fleabrain? Who is to say nay?

WONDER #2
THE CATACOMBS OF KOM EL SHOQAFA

FK:

We zoomed east across the Atlantic once again. For this flight, however, we departed at 10:00 P.M. in order to arrive while it was still dark. Fleabrain, prudent as always, had reminded me to bring a flashlight. Lightning and Alf were terrified and stayed outside, so we just peeked in and didn't remain long.

Catacomb means "underground cemetery," and it was first built in the second century AD. FB translated Kom el Shoqafa for me, which means "Mound of Shards" in Arabic. Relatives would gather to bury and remember their dead and have a bite to eat. But they were too superstitious to bring home their food vessels, FB explained, so they just broke them and left them behind.

I have tried to correct the color in my book using Burnt Sienna and Gray and Melon and Gold, but as I said, it was dark when we were there.

FB:
Oh, the melding of cultures—Greek, Roman, and Egyptian! The
carvings on the walls, the sarcophagi themselves, how artistically, historically, devastatingly fascinating!

But I didn't have time to present a proper lecture to Francine.

That lily-livered horse and the spineless hound were spooked by the spirit of a dead donkey, who, on September 28, 1900, caught his hoof in a crevice
and plunged to his
death to the bottom floor, thus introducing the catacombs to the modern world.

Alf's impatient whining and Lightning's terrified snorts slightly spoiled and definitely shortened the experience for us.

WONDER #3
THE LEANING TOWER OF PISA

FK:

Leaving Pittsburgh at 3:00 A.M., we arrived in Pisa at
9:00 A.M., just as the tourists were lining up. The Leaning Tower
of Pisa is a tall bell tower in the city of Pisa, Italy. The Leaning
Tower of Pisa leans. It really does. It made me sad to think about the
embarrassment of the poor architect who designed it long ago in the
twelfth century. Nobody is quite sure who he was, exactly, but he was
probably not very boastful about it. The Tower was built on a very
weak foundation, and when workers began the second floor, the Tower
began sinking into the soil, which was too soft on one side. They
did not try to build again for another hundred years, too busy with
wars. By the time they tried again, the soil had settled, and it was
much safer.

A young girl around my age fed Lightning a grape. I wanted to
converse, but I could not. One day I will learn Italian. Alf scampered
into the Tower, then up the stairs, before he was caught and returned
by an angry guard.

I have used White crayon with shades of Carnation Pink and
Silver to color the Tower in my book.

FB:

My heart mechanism was breaking for my Francine at the Leaning Tower of Pisa.

I was prepared to share a chuckle with her at the expense of the foolish designers of the Tower, but she was so solemn!

I pondered the situation and suddenly knew why. I am forthrightly sharing my intuition in this journal, for her to read.

Oh, Francine. I know it was the stairs, almost three hundred of them, which

you would never be able to climb (and I didn't dare carry you in public).

Three hundred stairs. When confronted with that reality up close, it must be hard.

And do not worry, Francine! I will teach you Italian.

What Lightning Knew

One week later, the tour of Wonders was finally over. Lightning and Alf and Franny and Fleabrain zoomed westward from Turkey, slowing down as they reached the Allegheny Plateau. There, beneath them, the Allegheny River from the northeast and Monongahela River from the southeast joined to form the mighty Ohio. Pittsburgh was a golden triangle floating in the waters. The city's bridges, rusted hulks during the day, shone like jeweled bracelets in the moonlight. Franny remembered a Truth of the Universe, as Fleabrain called them, a truth she'd never felt was very important Before.

"There's no place like home," she said. "Right, Fleabrain?"

That's what her father said every single time they returned from a summer visit to her grandparents in Michigan, or from a family get-together with her cousins in Brooklyn, New York. And, of course, that's what the intrepid Dorothy said in *The Wizard of Oz*, returning home to Kansas. Now, having traveled the world far and wide, having visited Wonder after Wonder all in one week, Franny decided that her own city was a Wonder, too, as she surveyed it from above with fresh, well-traveled eyes.

"Of course there's no place like home!" said Fleabrain. "But only on a purely rational level."

"Who decides these lists of Wonders, anyway? Couldn't everyone make up their own list of Wonders?" Franny asked.

Fleabrain chuckled. "That would certainly lead to a hodgepodge of lists, don't you think? Next thing you know, we'd have baseball fields and chewing-gum factories and the latest automobile on those lists! No, my dear, Wonders are Wonders because they are timeless, ancient, unique, and mysteriously beautiful."

"But why are there only seven Wonders? That's kind of limiting, don't you think?"

"I suppose there could be a few more than seven Wonders," replied Fleabrain, "but the ancient Greeks thought there were five planets, plus the Sun and the Moon. Ergo, seven, as they counted their own ancient Wonders. And, OK, OK—the Greeks were wrong about the number of planets, as we all know. But look at it this way: Seven is just the right amount for a week of wondrous sightseeing."

"I do think Pittsburgh is beautiful, though," said Franny.

"But that doesn't make one's home a Wonder!" snapped Fleabrain. "If everyone thought that, my dear, they'd hardly want to expand their vistas!"

"Oh, Fleabrain," said Franny. "I hope you don't think I'm ungrateful. It's just that coming home has made me see that my city is lovely, too, and that's a good thing. So, thank you."

"I have so many more true Wonders to show you!" said Flea-brain. "The Seven Wonders of the Oceans! The Seven Wonders of Outer Space! The Seven Wonders of each Continent! For every cele-bration, another tour of Wonders. Doesn't that sound Wonder-full?" Fleabrain gave a low chuckle, delighting in his own wit.

"I guess so," said Franny.

"Today will be a very busy day. We're behind in our travel journal entries. We certainly don't want our beautiful memories to be warped by time," Fleabrain said. "I believe the Taj Mahal should be White, with just a few shadowy touches of Maize and Sea Green, don't you? I would suggest a straightforward Tan crayon for both the Great Wall of China and the Roman Colosseum, the latter with a light wash of Silver."

Now the lights of Squirrel Hill were flickering beneath them. To Franny's great surprise, instead of returning to Frick Park and its stables, where her wheelchair was parked behind a boulder, Light-ning was circling the neighborhood, Alf close behind.

Fleabrain didn't seem to notice Lightning's detour. "As for the Hagia Sophia of Turkey," he was saying, "on the body of the mosque I believe you can be wildly artistic and use your Brick Red and Corn-flower crayons. For the minarets and dome—"

"Shh, Fleabrain," said Franny. "I need to concentrate on some-thing with Lightning right now, if you don't mind."

It had become clear to Franny lately that when a girl and a horse travel the Earth and night sky together, they become almost as one, naturally knowing one another's thoughts. She had leaned forward to hug Lightning, breathing in his sweet, horsey smell, and in that lovely, predawn moment, Lightning gave Franny his own gift. He began to share some secrets he held. But he wasn't really breaking any confidences. The few secrets Franny gleaned from Lightning were things she already knew yet hadn't really known she knew, until flying over the streets of Squirrel Hill early that morning.

In a corner house on Hobart Street, Walter Walter slept with his lucky buckeye, the one with the round yellow marking, under his pillow. He hoped its shining eye would protect him from enemies in the dark (mainly his angry father, who drank a lot). His brother, Seymour, was scared of rattlesnakes and atom bombs, which were easy to avoid in Squirrel Hill. He was also scared of thunder and their father, too, which weren't.

Inside their home on Douglas Street, A, B, and C Solomon envied the offspring of presidents, or the kids of any parents with good, secure positions, maybe with a bit of inherited money in the bank, to boot. Why couldn't their last name be Heinz or Mellon or Carnegie or Frick—rich people's names!—instead of Solomon? they wondered. Their dad had lost his job, and both parents were looking for work. When A, B, and C Solomon searched the streets for bottle caps, they were secretly hunting for change or for valuable arrowheads to pawn. When A, B, and C Solomon were invited to birthday parties, they usually sent their regrets. Birthday gifts were expensive.

On Phillips Avenue, more secrets:

Teresa Goodly felt dumb compared to Jane, and so she mimicked her older sister whenever possible. Jane's IQ was higher than Teresa's, she'd overheard her parents say. And little Rose wet her bed.

On Nicholson Street, Katy Green worried about her shyness, no longer a secret to Franny. Franny was her best friend, which wasn't a secret, either, but good to know for sure.

Now, swooping over Shady Avenue, Franny could hear Min sobbing in bed, muffling the sounds with her pillow. She was crying for Franny and Franny's condition; crying because her parents seemed to care more about Franny than her; crying because it was mean to feel bad about that. And did Franny herself still love her? she wondered. Crying, too, because she loved Milt the stable boy with all her heart, and he loved her back. Min and Milt. Milt and Min. Even their names were perfect together! But he was older than Min and would be going away to college in a year, probably forgetting all about her.

"Oh, Min," whispered Franny, her own heart aching with love for her sister. "Mom and Dad care about us both, even-steven." And she knew—she just knew—that Milt would never forget Min.

"Well, *I'm* not holding any secrets—you can be assured of that," said Fleabrain, guiltily remembering Zadie Ben's important Truth of the Universe he dared not share. "I am an open book, so to speak."

"Me, too," said Franny, although, truthfully, she was tired of visiting faraway Wonders. They made her feel lonely, somehow. She didn't want to hurt Fleabrain, who meant well. She would keep that feeling a secret.

But Lightning had learned something important during all his years of patient listening. Lightning knew that you didn't hold a secret; the secret held you. Until you told it to let you go.

Who Is the Gateway Angel?

Rag

un.
night,
morrow,
high 39. We.

Monday, March 9, 1953

WHO IS THE GATEWAY ANGEL?

by Jimmy Regis, Special Correspondent

The sleuths attempting to track down the young equestrian "angel" who this past December lit the star candle atop the Gateway Center Christmas tree (the very same "angel" who sang from her horse at the doorway to Mellon Bank) have come up empty-handed.

And who can explain the mysterious series of sonic booms this past week?

Naysayers declare that the sometimes-airborne, angelic-voiced creature was but a figment of our imaginations during an ecstatic holiday season. Yet others have identified her variously as Lucy Morgenstern, a teller at Mellon Bank, who has recently begun voice lessons; Rayelle Smith, an expert young equestrian from Shadyside; and Mrs. Lorne Grinstein's cousin Carol, visiting Squirrel Hill from Philadelphia, who is known for her practical jokes. All have denied the charges.

"I'm a good rider, but I'm not that good," says Miss Smith. "Anyway, I don't believe it really happened."

Yea-sayers disagree mightily, declaring they've recently witnessed an unidentified rider swooping across the night sky, almost too speedily to see. Others report various good deeds she continues to perform. For example, several long-lost items dropped down Pittsburgh chimneys (a wallet, dolls, a Remington electric shaver), and a grand piano appearing overnight in a ward of Children's Hospital. They're pretty sure the deeds are her doing.

"It is easy to imagine fantastic objects in the luminous Pittsburgh sky, lit up by the fires of the steel mills," chuckles Dr. Hornbill, astronomer at both the Allegheny Observatory and Buhl Planetarium.

Figment of our imaginations? Perhaps. But the phrase "seeing the Gateway Angel" has become a private joke among Pittsburghers, as well as a beauteous metaphor for the hopeful, can-do, modern spirit of our great town.

IV
SPRING 1953: HOPE

What the World Knew, Finally

Spring had always meant hope to Franny, for good times and imagined beginnings.

And hope really was a thing with feathers, as she had learned via Fleabrain from the poet Emily Dickinson. Soon the window screens would be carried up from the basement, and Franny would hear the birds of summer, the warblers and flycatchers and finches, hopefully winging their way toward Frick Park. Hope was also a faint smell, maybe just a promise, of lilacs in the air. Hope was the color green, a Crayola Spring Green, a faint flush on the lawns, green dots peppering the poplars and oaks. And hope was also the color black, as the slushy snow melted on stairs and porches, leaving the soot to be swept away.

Hope was a row of buckeyes on her windowsill, hard and strong for the springtime games.

And hope was KDKA radio blaring from a screened window. Another season for the Pittsburgh Pirates coming up! World Series, here we come! Hope, hope, hope!

Spring had always meant hope, but this spring, of course, was different. Hope was walking, if you could call it that, very slowly, in her braces, and only a few steps at a time.

But hope was also Squirrel Hill's very own Dr. Jonas Salk, who would be world-famous very soon.

"THE SCIENTIST SPEAKS FOR HIMSELF!" the newspapers announced excitedly. Dr. Jonas Salk would speak on CBS radio to the whole wide world, at exactly 10:45 P.M. on Thursday, March 26. A historic announcement on a historic day!

"I'm sure Katy's parents are letting her stay up to listen," Franny complained to her mother and father. "I don't see why you won't let me stay up, too."

"If Katy's parents allowed her to parachute from the Gulf Tower, does that mean we should, too? And you need more rest than Katy."

"Mom, I just want to hear his voice."

Her mother laid her hand gently on Franny's cheek. "Sweetheart, why is it so important to hear his voice? He'll be talking about the research at his lab, that's all. Some of what he says will be very technical."

Franny was surprised that her mother wasn't as jubilant as she was. She wondered if Dr. Salk's voice would sound like Rabbi Hailperin's, sonorously deep and wise. No, his voice would probably sound raspy, from all that cigarette smoking, although, of course, just as wise.

On the historic night of March 26, Franny was awakened in her bed by Salk's voice on the living room radio. She turned her head to look at her clock. The toe shoe of the dancer's bent leg pointed to eleven. The toe shoe of her stretched-out leg pointed gracefully toward nine. For fifteen whole minutes the voice rumbled wisely and hopefully. From her bedroom Franny could understand only one word, but it was an excellent word. *Progress!*

At the breakfast table the next morning, her parents were silent. Their eyes were red-rimmed and not exactly jubilant. "Good morning, girls!" they sang in one voice, a "Let's buck up and pretend to be happy" voice.

"What did Dr. Salk say?" Franny asked. "It was good news, right?"

Franny's mother looked down at her plate of eggs.

"It was good news, right?" Franny repeated. "Why so glum?"

"Yes," said her father. "A vaccine to prevent polio will be ready to be released to the world very soon, Salk said. The researchers know how to grow the virus, kill it, and use it to create a vaccine. They've already tested the vaccine on small groups. When those people were injected with the vaccine, even though the virus was dead, their bodies were fooled into producing antibodies against it, Salk and his team learned. Those antibodies would protect them if they were ever exposed to the live poliovirus. And nobody contracted polio after receiving the vaccine. In other words, the vaccine works and is safe. They will begin vaccinating large groups of kids next year, to further test the vaccine."

"He was so confident about the vaccine, he gave it to himself. Others in his lab injected themselves, too." Franny's mother's voice broke. "They say he even gave it to his own three sons."

Min slammed her fork down so hard, the plate holding her scrambled eggs broke into three pieces.

"That's not good news!" Min cried. "Why couldn't Salk have shared the vaccine with his neighbors, too? Did he have the vaccine last summer, before Franny got sick?"

"Oh, Min," said Mrs. Katzenback. Tears streamed from her eyes down to her nose. "You broke your plate," she said, as if that was the reason she was crying. She wiped her face with her hand and jumped up to remove the broken china and clumps of egg.

"Mom, I'm sorry," said Min. "I'll clean it up."

"No, no, I'll do it," said her mother, and Franny knew she wanted to continue crying in the kitchen.

Mr. Katzenback sat very still, as he always did when he was upset, his hands clasped tightly on the table.

"The vaccine to prevent polio is a little too late for our Franny," Mr. Katzenback said. "The researchers wanted to make very sure the vaccine was effective and safe before they gave it to the public. And we are happy for the kids who will be saved from polio with this vaccine. Very happy."

"But what about all those dimes pouring in from all over the country? Miles and miles of them! Weren't some of them being used to find a cure?" Franny asked. Deep down she knew the answer. Had she known all along? "Didn't Dr. Salk also talk about the cure he and his lab partners were working on?"

Her mother had returned with Min's scrambled eggs.

"There's no cure, Franny," Min whispered.

Mrs. Katzenback sat down slowly. "There is no cure for the

effects of the poliovirus, Franny," she said. "The virus attacked the motor neurons in your spinal cord. The resulting paralysis of your legs can't be undone."

"Francine," said her father. He always called her Francine at very serious moments. "Your family will be here to help you. And life goes on."

"You always say that," said Franny.

"Franny, please don't talk to your father that way," said Mrs. Katzenback. "He is trying so hard to make you understand."

"I will never understand!" Franny said. "And of course life goes on. Heck, easy for you to say! Your lives go on as pedestrians! Mine goes on in a wheelchair!"

"But exercise and massage *are* helping you," said her mother. "You're beginning to walk! And please don't say 'heck.'"

"Exercise and massage take too long! And who says they're helping me? I'm not *really* walking. If that's walking, then I like my wheelchair much, much better. Furthermore, it feels good to say 'heck'! Heck, heck, heck!"

"I personally think Franny should be allowed to say 'heck' as many times as she wants to," said Min. "And I'll say it, too. HECK!"

"A million times 'heck'!" shouted Franny.

Her parents looked at one another and smiled, even though now her father was crying, too. He reached over to hold his wife's hand. "Muriel, under the circumstances, I think we should allow our daughters this particular transgression."

There was a game Franny liked to play. She'd repeat the most gorgeous words she could think of, words like *sassafras* and *gladiola* and *filigree*, over and over and over again, until the beautiful words were transformed into meaningless, nonsense syllables, having lost all of their luster. *Heck*, which wasn't exactly beautiful to begin with, had easily met the same fate. And saying the word didn't make her feel better. Not really.

That same evening, her parents were visiting relatives, and Min had plans to meet her friends at Weinstein's Restaurant. Min was wearing Orange Spice lipstick and her good blue angora cardigan, which meant Milt was probably one of the friends, maybe even the only friend. Nurse Olivegarten would be staying with Franny for the evening. Franny had begged to stay alone, but her parents had absolutely refused.

"Franny, do you want me to stay home with you?" Min asked.

"That's OK," said Franny. She'd try not to be a baby. And she did understand about boyfriends. Anyway, Nurse Olivegarten would be spending the whole night on the telephone. She could pretend she was alone.

Franny pored over the newspaper. Maybe she'd discover a piece of information her parents had missed. Her heart pounded as she read, *A polio-free world may be at the fingertips of a Pittsburgh scientist* . . . But the news report was about vaccines and prevention. Not one single word about curing those already stricken.

Aren't I a part of the world? she thought.

Suddenly, a chemical whiff of lilacs. Nurse Olivegarten.

"Your parents told me you were a bit upset today," said Nurse Olivegarten, standing at the edge of the living room. "They said you had been expecting the announcement of a cure for polio." Nurse

Olivegarten's ruby red lips twitched into a little smile. "Oh, my dear, dear girl. I'm so sorry you misunderstood Salk's work. Perhaps this has been the problem all along."

"What do you mean?" Franny asked.

Nurse Olivegarten moved closer to Franny. "You've been waiting for a quick cure, eh? That's why you haven't been working hard enough at your physical therapy. Nothing is easy. Everything takes work."

"*I have* worked at it. But I'm tired of work," Franny said. Then she whispered, "I'm only eleven."

"I beg your pardon? What did you say?"

"I'm tired of work."

"When I was your age, I certainly wasn't afraid of work! I sold carrots and fiddleheads at my grandfather's farm stand in New Brunswick, Canada. I scrubbed a kitchen floor every now and then, too. One is *never* too young to work, young lady."

"This isn't carrots. This isn't fiddleheads," said Franny. Whatever those were. A Canadian vegetable, probably.

Nurse Olivegarten's lips twitched again. "My dear girl, don't you want to be like all the other kids, instead of a cripple? Don't you want to keep up with them when you go back to school?"

"Yes."

"Well, I want to get you out of that awful, confining chair. It won't be easy, and, yes, it will take work. But isn't that what you want? To walk again?"

"I guess so."

"You *guess* so!"

Franny was silent. She felt so tired.

"I think we should practice now, as a matter of fact, to get your motivation back."

"I don't really want to," Franny said.

"I said *now*," declared Nurse Olivegarten, looming over Franny. "It's only seven in the evening." Suddenly Franny felt very small. The nurse put her arms under Franny's armpits and jerked her up from the wheelchair. "Go ahead! Just as we practiced this morning."

Lean on left foot. Swing right hip out. Step with right foot.

Lean on right foot. Swing left hip out. Step with left foot.

Over and over and over. Franny's tiredness became pain. "Enough," she said, crying now.

"Again," said Nurse Olivegarten. "Practice makes perfect."

Lean on left foot. Swing right hip out. Step with right foot.

Lean on right foot. Swing left hip out. Step with left foot.

"No more," Franny said when they reached her chair again.

"Again!" said Nurse Olivegarten. She squeezed Franny's arm, leaving the marks of her ruby red nails, like tiny mean smiles.

Franny's pain had become anger. "No!" she shouted, sitting in her chair and rolling herself toward her bedroom. "No more!"

FB Saliva #2-X

Fleabrain felt the venom rising within him, his most potent concoction yet: FB Saliva #2-X, a fast-acting and effective version of FB Saliva #2, formulated for larger entities. Quivering, he sat on top of Sparky's Finest, waiting. Alf awoke, sensing that something interesting was brewing between Fleabrain and Franny.

"Nurse Olivegarten!" Franny called. "Please come here!"

As usual, Nurse Olivegarten made Franny call her more than once.

"Nurse Olivegarten!"

The nurse spoke from behind the closed door. "What is it?"

"Please come in. I want to ask you something."

Nurse Olivegarten stepped into the room. "I think I've had enough of your unpleasantness for the evening."

Franny was sitting in her wheelchair by her night table. She took a deep breath, then asked her question. "Why do you hurt me?"

Nurse Olivegarten flushed. "Practicing hurts. Practicing something hard always hurts."

"No, not practicing. You know what I mean."

"I don't think I do."

"You hurt me on purpose, just because your method isn't working. I'm telling."

"I don't know what you are going to 'tell.'"

"Oh, yes, you do," said Franny.

Nurse Olivegarten's eyes were narrow green slits. She loomed in front of Franny now, arms akimbo. "I am helping you. Your parents know that."

"You aren't helping me. And my parents don't know everything," said Franny, her voice trembling.

On the night table a magnified Fleabrain suddenly appeared behind Sparky's Finest. Franny reached for the bottle cap and placed it behind her eyeglass lens.

"My parents don't know everything!" Franny repeated, louder and braver. And then she instructed, "Make her smaller than a mouse but bigger than a gnat!"

Fleabrain's leg gave a "thumbs"-up wriggle.

"My dear girl, what are you talking about?" asked Nurse Olivegarten.

"Actually, the size of a large spider will do," said Franny.

"*What* are you talking about? Eh?"

Fleabrain bit Nurse Olivergarten behind each of her ears. *Pffft!* There was the pungent smell of firecrackers and popcorn, mingled with that of decaying lilacs.

"Eh?

Eh?

Eh?"

Three seconds was all it took. A miniaturized Nurse Olivegarten now stood at the tip of Franny's clodhopper shoe, the nurse's mouth wide open in astonishment.

Franny leaned over to get a good look at this tiny being, a squeaking, quaking specimen of Nurse Olivegarten. How wonderful to be looking down at her instead of up! Franny felt huge and strong and free.

"Well? How does it feel to be smaller than me?" Franny asked.

It would have been so easy to squash her, but Franny just couldn't.

Nurse Olivegarten turned and ran. She raced around the treelike legs of the bed and tripped over the rolling mountain ranges of the braided rug. Righting herself, she galloped toward the bottom shelf of Franny's bookcase and disappeared behind *Anne of Green Gables*. Franny wheeled over and shook each book until a wailing Nurse Olivegarten was finally dislodged from *Treasure Island*, Chapter IX. Franny reached out to break her fall, catching one of her tiny legs as she floated to the floor, but Nurse Olivegarten wriggled away. She ran toward the bed again, hurling herself beneath it.

Franny leaned down to see, as far as she could. Nurse Olivegarten was hanging on to a bedspring with both hands. Alf scurried under the bed and tried to bring her down with his paw.

"Alf, no!" yelled Franny.

But Alf's hunting instincts were aroused by this strange,

uniform-clad insect, who was now pulling herself from spring to spring like a monkey-bars champion. The dog scurried after her, crawling on his belly from one end of the bed to the other, until Nurse Olivegarten, exhausted, dropped to the floor.

"No!" cried Franny.

But there was no stopping Alf. His big tongue hanging out, he joyfully leaped toward Nurse Olivegarten and slurped her up. Triumphantly, Alf emerged from under the bed. Around and around the room the dog raced, his prey's little upper body hanging from his dripping mouth, her little arms gesticulating wildly.

"Alf, drop it! Drop it!" Franny yelled.

Alf obediently deposited Nurse Olivegarten at the foot of Franny's wheelchair, just as his proud, wagging tail (with Fleabrain on it, enjoying the spectacle) got tangled in the wire of the ballerina alarm clock, which crashed to the floor. The clock's protective glass cover popped out, as did its innards, to the off-key, dying strains of the *Moonlight Sonata*.

The ballerina, or what was left of her, stared reproachfully at Franny, as if to say, "I am but an innocent victim of this terrible ruckus; I, who have always performed my strenuous job so heroically, especially at noon and midnight!" The dancer's graceful arms and legs were scattered nearby, like a game of pickup sticks.

Meanwhile, Franny realized that tiny Nurse Olivegarten had fled across the room to the window and was at that moment pulling herself up the curtains, hand over hand.

"Nurse Olivegarten! Wait!" hollered Franny. "Fleabrain, quickly! We need to reverse the miniaturization process!"

But it was too late. The tiny nurse reached the sill, dived through a hole in the screen, and disappeared into the night.

Franny felt terrible. No matter how much she disliked and feared Nurse Olivegarten, no matter what Nurse Olivegarten had done, no living being, large or small, deserved such an unnatural transformation.

"Don't worry," said Fleabrain. "Nurse Olivegarten will be all right."

"Fleabrain, what are you saying?" asked Franny. "How can she survive on the streets, as small as she is?"

"She will. Trust me."

"But how do you *know*?"

Fleabrain seemed to be averting his tiny eyes on either side of his head. "I just know," he said evasively. "Nurse Olivegarten will be fine, although she doesn't deserve to be." As if to change the subject, he added, "I can certainly fix that alarm clock. I'll have your ballerina dancing in no time. A simple task. I'll start working on it pronto."

And then the question came to Franny, a question as natural and inevitable as the air in the room.

"Oh, Fleabrain, can you please fix me, too?"

The Good News and the Bad

Fleabrain raised one of his legs in a "Just a minute, please" gesture to Franny's question. He was at that moment using his tubelike mouthparts to screw the ballerina's arms and legs onto the clock's face. He had already replaced the clock's innards, and once the limbs were connected, he lifted the glass front piece onto the clock, jumping up and down on it to snap it into place.

"Done!" he declared as the dancer's outstretched "minute leg" began to move. "All fixed."

"Fleabrain, did you hear my question?" asked Franny.

"Oops—one second while I adjust the appendages to the correct time, according to my instincts." Fleabrain turned the clock's back knob to set the ballerina's legs at thirty-five minutes past eight. "Now," he said, "where were we?"

"I asked you a question," said Franny. "An important one."

"Oh. You did?"

"Yes. I want to know if you could fix me with your potions, being as wise and expert and powerful as you are."

"Oh. Right. Let me ponder on that." Fleabrain reclined on top of the clock, put several tarsi over his face, and pondered. After a few seconds he looked up and asked, "Do you want the long answer or the short answer?"

"Both," said Franny.

"Do you want the good news or the bad news?"

"Both," said Franny. "You're stalling."

"Me? Stalling? OK. The good news is that Nurse Olivegarten will be all right."

"You told me that already. What's the bad news?"

"The good news is also the bad news. Nurse Olive will be 'all right,' as in back-to-her-full-size-sour-self, with only the occasional nightmare or intrusive memory."

"I don't get it," said Franny.

Fleabrain looked sheepish. "The power of my potions is temporary, dear Francine. The effect disappears eventually, just like a fleabite. Only the memory of the experience remains. I don't have to reverse the process; it happens by itself, naturally."

"You reversed the process when you miniaturized *me*."

"Yes, well—I pretended to reverse it, purely for the dramatic effect. I wanted you to believe I was all-powerful. You would have returned to your regular size on your own."

"Oh." Francine was beginning to understand the import of what Fleabrain was saying. Her insides suddenly filled up with a great sadness, crowding out her one last hope.

"So even if I were able to concoct a fluid to enliven the nerves in your legs and strengthen your muscles, thus enabling you to walk and run and skip and dance, my dear, dear Francine, it wouldn't last. And what you are asking me to do is so very, very complicated! I predict that humans will be walking on the moon itself years before your difficult problem is solved by scientists!"

"Now you're exaggerating," said Franny.

"Perhaps," said Fleabrain. "So . . . the long answer is also the short answer. I can't fix you. I'm so, so sorry."

"What about time travel?" asked Franny.

"What about it?"

"What if you do something powerful and magical and somehow we both go back in time to the exact moment when I got polio, whenever and wherever it was. And somehow the danger is averted, and I don't come down with polio, and things go on the way they were meant to? How about *that*, Fleabrain?"

Fleabrain seemed to smile ruefully. "Time travel is impossible."

"Who says it is?"

"I do. I am smart enough to know that Time Past is just a memory, not a real place. There is no 'it' to go back to, Francine."

Maybe it was the slight condescension in Fleabrain's tone, or her huge disappointment in Fleabrain's non-all-powerfulness, or the fatigue of a long, sad day, but Franny was angrier than she'd ever been in her entire eleven years.

"You are a sham, Fleabrain," she said. "Just like the Wizard of Oz!"

Sham, sham, sham, Fleabrain, the taunting chorus sang.

Fleabrain hung his head mournfully. "I admit to a bit of shamming," he said.

"Actually, it's even worse, Fleabrain," said Franny. "You're prob-ably not even real. You could be just a figment of my imagination."

Fleabrain lifted his head. "Now, *that* hurts, Francine. It really does. I am at your service, but I belong to nobody but myself!"

"Oh, Fleabrain. I'm sorry," said Franny, leaning very close to him to look into his tiny eyes as best she could. "I didn't mean to hurt your feelings. It's just that I'm very upset. Of course you're real. But I wish you'd told me the truth. You must have known, being so miraculously smart, that if *you* couldn't fix me, then neither could Dr. Salk."

"Do you really wish I'd told you the truth? That unhappy truth would have spoiled all the fun, Francine!"

"'Fun'? Was it all about having fun? I thought we were friends, Fleabrain."

"Of course, of course, of course we're friends! But didn't we *both* have fun, my dear, dear Francine?" Fleabrain's little voice was shriller than usual as he leaped back and forth across the top of the ballerina alarm clock. "And there's still more fun to have. Oh, the Wonders I've yet to show you! Bug it, listen to me, Francine. We can't go back in time, but we can do something better. We can stay young! I've just finished *Ulysses*, that wonderful book by the great Irish writer James Joyce, born February 2, 1882, died January 13, 1941. The main character has a lollapalooza of an idea. Listen, please, to this magnif-icent quote!"

Waving a tarsus dramatically, Fleabrain closed his tiny eyes and began to orate:

"Somewhere in the east: early morning: set off at dawn. Travel round in front of the sun, steal a day's march on him. Keep it up for ever never grow a day older technically . . ."

"What do you think of that?" Fleabrain asked hopefully, opening his eyes. "You and I and Lightning and Alf will just keep traveling in front of the sun for perpetuity and never grow old! Technically."

"I think it's a stupid idea!" said Franny. "Who wants to stay the same age? I want to grow up, like every other kid in Squirrel Hill. I want to stay in Squirrel Hill, too. I don't want to see any more faraway Wonders. Not yet, anyway."

"'Stupid'? The great James Joyce, stupid? And, by implication, myself? Ha!" cried Fleabrain, stung by Franny's insult and momentarily forgetting what they were arguing about. "The great James Joyce and I can't be any stupider than What's-His-Name, the author of that book about Charlotte and Gilbert that you love so much."

Fleabrain caught his breath, immediately realizing, by the stricken expression on Franny's face, that he'd gone too far.

"What did you just say?" asked Franny.

"I'm so sorry, Francine. I meant no offense!" Fleabrain spluttered.

"Whom did you say *Charlotte's Web* was about?"

"Charlotte the spider and Gilbert the pig."

"For your information, the pig's name is Wilbur."

"Wilbur, then. A similar name and a momentary forgetfulness."

"Fleabrain, you have a terrific memory, and you know it. How can you forget something as important as a main character's name? I bet you never even read *Charlotte's Web*!"

"Of course I read it!"

"Well, let's just see about that." Franny picked up a pencil and *Charlotte's Web* from the night table and flipped through its pages. "Here is a little pop quiz for you."

"Are you saying you don't trust that I've read it?" Fleabrain asked. There seemed to be tiny beads of sweat on his tubelike mouthparts.

"That's exactly what I'm saying," said Franny, pursing her lips. "OK. First question. Where does the book take place?"

Fleabrain took a deep breath. "I believe it takes place on a farm. Somewhere in Pennsylvania."

"One-half point for an incomplete answer. Near what city?"

"I don't recall."

"Many readers may not have remembered that detail. But I would have thought *you* would, smarty-pants."

"I resent your tone, Francine."

"I apologize. Next question. The girl's name?"

"Phyllis."

"Wrong. The rat's name?"

"Al."

"Wrong. The rhinoceros's name?"

"Uh, Slim?"

"There's no rhinoceros in the story, Fleabrain," said Franny sadly. She was getting no satisfaction at all from Fleabrain's humiliation.

"Trick question!" Fleabrain protested.

Franny ignored him. "Explain the use of 'radiant' in *Charlotte's Web*."

"Ah!" said Fleabrain. "*Radiant:* adjective. 1. Exhibiting happiness, joy, hope, love, liveliness, et cetera. 2. Radiating light beams; reflecting rays of light. 3. *Physics:* transmitted by radiation; *radiant* energy. *Radiant:* noun: that which radiates; as: a. *Optics.* The object or point from which light emanates. b. *Astronomy.* The point in the heavens at which, when traced backward, the visible paths of meteors appear to meet. And, of course, *radiant:* synonym: see *bright.*"

"Fine, that's the by-heart dictionary definition. But what's so important about the word in Wilbur's story?"

Fleabrain paused. "I don't recall."

"Who was Zuckerman?"

"I have no idea."

"What happened at the fairgrounds?"

"Rides? Bake sales?"

"Something important happened there, Fleabrain."

"I don't recall."

"What is Charlotte's *magnum opus*?"

"Latin for 'great work.'"

"Yes, we both know you're a scholarly classicist, Fleabrain. But what's the meaning of *magnum opus* in this story?"

"No idea."

"And, final question, how does the book end?"

Fleabrain bent his head. "Let me ponder upon that," he said. A full minute slowly ticked by, announced by the click of the ballerina's pointed toe.

Fleabrain lifted his head and whispered, "I . . . I don't know."

"Oh, Fleabrain," said Franny, at last. "You've failed the test, of course. One-half point out of ten."

"Wasn't the brilliant French scholar Rashi, short for **RA**bbi **SH**lomo **YI**tzchaki, born February 22, 1040, died July 13, 1105, commended for saying 'I don't know'? Why can't I, Fleabrain, say 'I don't know' every now and then?"

Franny tossed her pencil across the room in exasperation. "Rashi was being humble. You weren't being humble, Fleabrain. You just didn't read the book."

"I admit I leafed through the book quickly. I didn't peruse it in depth. OK, I only looked at the terrific illustrations by the American artist Garth Williams, born April 16, 1912."

"Just as I suspected," said Franny. Her eyes filled with tears.

"To quote Anonymous, don't you agree that 'a picture is worth a thousand words'?"

"Not the words of *Charlotte's Web*, Fleabrain! You criticized someone very important to me and you didn't even know her."

"May I interject and point out that Charlotte is fictional?" said Fleabrain diffidently.

"Sure, she's fictional. But to me, she's *real*! I know that sounds odd, but that's the way I feel. And you weren't honest with me. Friends are honest with one another."

"I'll read it tonight. I promise, Francine. You can test me again tomorrow."

"But you've failed the friendship test, Fleabrain." Franny stared down at her shoes. She could hardly bear to look at him.

"Please understand, Francine. There were so many other books I wanted to read in depth. Important tomes! Classics of the ages!"

At that, Franny slowly reached up to remove Sparky's Finest from in front of her eye. She stared down at the bottle cap in her palm, then closed her fingers around it. She lifted her arm.

"You've broken my heart, Fleabrain," Franny said.

"No, wait, Francine! Please don't! I apologize with every cell of my own pumping mechanism! Test me tomorrow!"

But Francine swung her arm, her pitcher's arm, and the bottle cap flew like her special fastball, bright beams of energy following its flight. When Sparky's Finest hit the wall, its surface became a web of cracks, which shattered into shards of radiant light.

"Oh, Fleabrain," Franny whispered. She began to cry. "No more tomorrows."

Reading

B ut, of course, tomorrow came.

As the velvet gray light of dawn curtained the vast Pittsburgh sky, Fleabrain finished reading the last page of *Charlotte's Web.*

He immediately decided to write his opinion of the book in Franny's journal.

He had to search for the journal. He finally found it at the bottom of her closet, buried under her clodhopper shoes and a few items her parents had forgotten to burn—an old, naked doll, puzzles with missing pieces, and a twisted Slinky.

You were correct, Francine!
I quite enjoyed the book!

The author demonstrates a way with words,
acute powers of observation,
sprightly humor,

and
an understanding of a young person's world.

Bravo, American writer Elwyn Brooks (aka E. B.)
White! (July 11, 1899–)

Professor Doctor Gutman
and the Pack

I've just received a very strange phone call from Nurse Olivegarten," said Franny's mother, later that Saturday morning. "She is moving to a small town in New Brunswick, Canada, and quitting all of her home nursing assignments, effective immediately. Something about needing time to reflect upon life's path."

"Really?" asked Franny, her heart leaping.

She was sitting on the front porch with Katy and Professor Doctor Gutman, who was helping them practice a duet for trombone and clarinet. "Did her voice . . . Did she sound OK?"

"Yes, I think so," said Mrs. Katzenback. "Although she seemed a bit subdued. I wonder why she couldn't reflect upon life's path in Pennsylvania."

"I mean, did her . . . her voice sound peculiarly small and squeaky?" Franny asked. "You can tell a lot from a person's voice," she hurriedly added.

Her mother gave Franny a quizzical look. "No. Why should her voice sound small and squeaky?"

"Oh, no reason," said Franny, relieved. "Well, I guess Nurse Olivegarten left because she missed her family."

"Or maybe she missed the fiddleheads," said Katy, who knew some of the story.

At that, the two girls collapsed into a fit of giggles. Katy put her nose into her trombone bell to stem the laughter, which made a hollow, honking noise, and that only made them both laugh harder. Professor Doctor Gutman and Mrs. Katzenback raised their eyebrows at one another. But Franny could tell they were both pleased to hear the laughter, especially hers. She herself had been subdued and sad after Dr. Salk's historic yet disappointing announcement to the world. Of course, the news was only disappointing to Franny and others who had been hoping for a cure. The rest of the world was rejoicing. But now she was rejoicing because of her mother's news!

"Nurse Olivegarten did leave us in a bit of a lurch," said her mother. "Although I suppose your father and I can help you with the exercises until we find another professional."

"And before you know it, September will be here again. Franny will be back in school every day, and the problem will be solved," Katy said.

Katy. Dear, dear Katy.

"Back in school. Problem solved," said Franny. What beautiful words those were.

She lifted her clarinet to her mouth and created a tune for that refrain on the spot. *Back in school. Problem solved.* Six tuneful toots.

"Excellent," said Professor Doctor Gutman. "Katy, can you play a D along with Franny at the end of that refrain? Sit up straight now to get lots of air into your lungs."

Katy on trombone wasn't quiet. Katy on trombone was earsplitting and cacophonous. The loud *wa-wa* wail of her instrument easily drowned out Franny's clarinet.

Most likely attracted by the toots and wailing of the girls' duet, the Pack had turned down Shady Avenue. It was prime bottle-cap hunting season. The melting snow revealed treasures buried during the colder months, and each member of the Pack was carrying their cap sack.

"Howdy," said Walter Walter.

But Walter Walter was staring at Professor Doctor Gutman, as were the others—A, B, and C, Teresa, Seymour, and Rose.

"Thank you for doing such good work in your science lab," said B, in a hushed, respectful voice. The others nodded their heads.

Professor Doctor Gutman smiled modestly.

Continuing to stare, the Pack stood at the foot of the walk, clutching their bags.

Franny knew why they were staring, of course. Professor Doctor Gutman was now an honored and official neighborhood celebrity. There had been photos of Salk's team in the local newspapers, including Shady Avenue's own Professor Doctor Gutman, standing right at the elbow of the great Dr. Jonas Salk. No one in the Pack had yet caught sight of Salk in the flesh, even though he lived somewhere in the neighborhood, but here, in front of them, was Salk's esteemed colleague. That was almost as exciting as seeing the great Dr. Jonas

Salk himself. There was a golden aura surrounding the professor, like sunshine after a dark, frightening thunderstorm. And the Pack was made up of the very kids the researchers had been working so hard to save from the scourge of polio.

"Well, see you, Franny. See you, Katy," said Teresa, as they all turned to continue their bottle-cap hunt. "We miss you, Franny!"

"Wait a minute, Ter," said Franny.

"What?" asked Teresa, turning around.

"Come back here for a sec," Franny said.

Teresa frowned and went to stand at the foot of Franny's front walk again. The rest of the Pack followed.

"Why do you always say that?" Franny asked.

"Say what?"

"'We miss you, Franny,' as if I've gone away, or something."

"Just being nice."

"It's not so nice when the person you miss is right here in front of you."

"You know what I mean, Franny."

"Actually," said Franny, "I don't. This is me, and I'm here."

Teresa rubbed her toe in a sidewalk crack. "It's the polio. You know. You're contagious, Franny."

"I've told you over and over. I'm *not* contagious," Franny said.

"Well, Jane says polio is contagious where kids are concerned. She says she knows that for a verified fact."

Professor Doctor Gutman cleared his throat. He leaned over the porch railing, his hand under his chin. His black bristly eyebrows were raised in disapproval.

"Tell me," he asked, "who is this Jane?"

"My older sister," said Teresa.

"How much older?" asked the professor.

"She's in seventh grade."

"Is Jane a scientist?"

"Yes. No. Well, she plans to be, but she isn't yet, I guess," Teresa said, looking uncomfortable. "She has a very high IQ."

"Do us a favor, please," said Professor Doctor Gutman in his deep, rumbly voice. "Tell Jane of the high IQ that you've spoken to a certified scientist today. Tell her he told you something important." Professor Doctor Gutman stared piercingly at each Pack member in turn. "And it's this . . ." His large hand, gold wedding band glinting, reached for Franny's. "Your sister does not know of what she is speaking. People who have been infected with the poliovirus are contagious for only a short period, and for Franny, that period has ended. Her immune system developed its own antibodies to kill the poliovirus in her body— unfortunately, not before the virus had already done its damage. But Franny is *not* contagious! Would you kindly tell that to Jane, please?"

Franny's eyes filled with tears. She held on to the professor's hand.

Teresa grinned. "Sure. I'll tell that to Jane."

"Right. She's not contagious," confirmed Katy. "And she's my best friend."

Walter Walter looked at Franny. Franny looked back.

Come on, Double-Dose Walter Walter, Franny thought. *I know you. You don't need your lucky buckeye or garlic or your father or your brother to help you do what's right.*

Walter Walter strolled up to the porch. "I have some questions," he said.

"No, *I* have a question, Professor!" Seymour called out. "You're not an American. Are you still spying? Will you be selling U.S. secrets to foreign countries?"

"Oh, pipe down, Seymour," said Walter Walter. "He's a hero, not a spy, you noodlehead!"

"Whether or not I myself am an American," said Professor Doctor Gutman, still holding Franny's hand, "or a hero, or even a spy, is entirely beside the point. This girl was infected by the poliovirus, but she is no longer contagious."

"Hey, would you swear to God about that?" Teresa asked.

Professor Doctor Gutman's mouth twitched. A sort-of smile. If Franny had blinked, she would have missed it. She hoped Professor Doctor Gutman wasn't going to say swearing to God was entirely beside the point. Teresa placed great stock in swearing to God.

"Yes, I would," said Professor Doctor Gutman.

"Good," said Teresa. "I'll tell Jane that, too."

"And, all of you, tell your parents, as well. They should have known this themselves." Professor Doctor Gutman turned to Walter Walter. "Now, young man, do you have some questions for me?"

"Actually, my questions are for Franny," Walter Walter said.

"Me?" Franny asked.

Walter Walter grinned. "Are the buckeyes I gave you ready for the tournaments?"

"You bet," said Franny. "And thank you for the twenty-one Get Well cards."

Walter Walter blushed, glanced at his brother quickly, then looked back at Franny. "And, hey, what about your pitching arm? Still good?"

Franny squinted and put a finger to her head, pretending to think hard. *"Was mich nicht umbringt, macht mich stärker,"* she said.

Professor Doctor Gutman looked up at the sky and roared with laughter.

"Huh?" said Walter Walter.

"German," said Franny. "It means 'better than ever.'"

Rereading

George Gutman was rereading Kafka's *Die Verwandlung*. He often reread books. Sometimes, while rereading, he was shocked to discover that a book had magically changed. It was as if the author had tiptoed into the professor's library, plucked the book off the shelf, and created a brand-new one, without changing a single word.

Before, the story about a man who turned into a big ugly bug had filled the professor with the pain of a hard truth. Life was silly and meaningless. The death of loved ones, meaningless. It was not a story he enjoyed reading. Before.

Today, the story was making him laugh. Imagine that, thought the professor, wiping his eyes. A man wakes up, and he's changed into a bug. Horrible! But what will happen next? You must carry on to find out. You turn the page and continue the story, trying very hard to make sense of it. You turn more pages and . . . surprise! The book is funny. After a while, it's even beautiful.

Rereading

Dearest Francine,
Hi, there!
Me again.
Haven't dropped you a line in a while.
I've
been busy!
I
just want to tell you that I've reread Charlotte's Web.
I've
never done that, reread a whole book, although I admit
to rereading sections of Paramoigraphy. But there are so
many books to read. Why
waste time rereading?

Nevertheless, I did reread Charlotte's Web. After this
reading, I have distilled the book down to
two important Truths of the Universe:

(1) It's fun to be a writer, as Charlotte was.

(2) Friendship is important in life, which, of course, reinforced what I already knew.

(There was a third, minor TOTU:

(3) Eat a good breakfast. That pig could sure pack it in.)

Francine, I believe I am a good writer.
Charlotte's style was
spare and poetic, using only a word or two crafted inside her web
to stunning effect!
I admire that. I can't decide on my own style,
or
what I would consider
my magnum opus.
But I am industriously working on:

twelve sonnets, two historical novels, fifty haiku, one comedy of manners à la the English novelist Jane Austen (December 16, 1775–July 18, 1817), seven romantic poems combining the styles of the great Persian poet Rumi (September 30, 1207–December 17, 1273) and the Chilean poet Pablo Neruda (born July 12, 1904), a tale of horror à la the American writer Edgar Allan Poe (January 19, 1809–October 7, 1849), a dissertation on the causes of the

Spanish-American War, and the libretto for a possible
opera or Broadway musical.

One other thing. I thought I was a good friend.
I guess I was mistaken.

I WILL TRY HARDER! I WILL BE THE BEST FRIEND IN
THE UNIVERSE!
No more show-offy shamming.

But how can I be a good friend

if you won't let me?
Yours everlastingly,
FB

The Buckeye Amendments

Teresa Goodly imagined the story and told it to the others. Teresa's story was inspired by Mrs. Nelson, who got the information from her anthropologist husband, who said that children in the British Commonwealth played the same buckeye game as the Pack in Squirrel Hill. Across oceans and throughout time, Mrs. Nelson said, young people have always learned from one another.

"Here's the story," Teresa said. "One hundred years ago, a family sailed to America from England or Ireland, or maybe it was Scotland. They settled in Squirrel Hill, in the days when the chattering gray squirrel roamed the land, stealing grain from the settlers and raining nuts on their roofs. The brother and the sister greatly missed their native land, with its shady horse chestnut trees and cool rivers. They were always moping about, bored and crabby, until one day their mother shook a broom at them, saying, 'Get ye out of the house!' So the brother and the sister moseyed over to Homewood Cemetery that autumn day. They noticed the fallen round nuts beneath a buckeye tree, reminding them of the nuts of the horse chestnut trees of their homeland and the games they used to play with them. The ancestors of those siblings, and the ancestors' neighbors, have been playing the buckeye game around here ever since."

That was Teresa's story, and the Pack agreed it was a good one, and quite plausible. They also agreed on the rules of the Buckeye Tournaments, which they'd been playing for years and knew by heart. But that spring, Teresa posted the rules on the bulletin board of Sol's Ye Olde Candy Shoppe, adding some important amendments written in Brick Red crayon for emphasis.

PRELIMINARIES OF THE GAME

1. In the autumn, gather a bunch of round buckeyes that have fallen to the ground from the buckeye trees of Homewood Cemetery. Divide them up among the Pack. Note: Use a penknife to pry apart the sharp casing to get to the buckeye inside. Better than a potato peeler! Carol, THIS ONE'S FOR YOU. Remember last autumn's skin loss?

2. Put a hole through each buckeye. You can use a screwdriver or a nail. Do this carefully so the buckeye does not split.

3. Keep your buckeyes indoors ALL winter.

4. In the spring, thread an old shoelace through the hole of each buckeye. Knot it at the end. Take your buckeye(s) outdoors for tournaments.

THE GAME
Objective

To crack the buckeye of the opposing player, or make it fall to the ground.

Play

1. *Two buckeye players face off, holding one buckeye each on its string.*

2. *One buckeye player is defense, and just stands there. The player on offense swings, trying to crack the other's buckeye, and wins the match if this happens. If no one wins that round, just keep going until someone does, alternating offense and defense.*

3. *The buckeye with the most winning matches compared to his opponent always goes first. If both are playing their first match of the season or the buckeyes are tied, you flip a coin.*

Scoring

The winning buckeye is a King-over-1, if it is the first match of the season. After its next winning match, it is a King-over-2, et cetera. Last year Seymour's buckeye was a King-over-50. No buckeye in history has ever scored that high. Some kids swear it never happened, since scoring is based on the honor system. Some say it happened because of the vinegar. (See Amendment #1.)

IMPORTANT AMENDMENTS TO THE RULES!

Buckeye Amendment #1, Spring 1953

Players are forbidden to bake their buckeyes or soak them in vinegar over the winter. This makes buckeyes as hard as concrete and unbeatable. What if we all did that? What would be the point of the game?

Buckeye Amendment #2, Spring 1953

If one player is in a wheelchair, the other player may (or may not) sit in a chair, too, to create a level playing ground. It's up to you. Lawn chairs give the best spring.

One of Franny's buckeyes was King-over-24 by mid-April, as was Seymour's. On the day of Franny's challenge, they faced off in front of the Walters' porch on Hobart Street. The whole Pack and some stragglers from other blocks were there. So was Alf, and, therefore, Fleabrain.

"Go, Franny!" whispered Fleabrain.

Seymour won the coin flip and decided to stand rather than sit. He flexed his buckeye arm, then gave Franny a piercing look, his infamous "Seymour eye," which had intimidated many a lesser player. Franny was ready for him, her King-over-24 hanging firm on its shoelace.

Seymour raised his arm, then stopped suddenly, midswing.

"I think I'll sit down," he said.

Walter Walter carried down his grandmother's red-and-white-striped lawn chair from his front porch.

"You're making a big mistake," Teresa called out. "Standing is better for hitting. You're not used to sitting, Seymour."

"Pipe down," said Seymour, sitting down on the lawn chair. He raised his arm and swung, missing Franny's buckeye. "Do-over, do-over!" Seymour shouted. "I'm not used to sitting."

"No do-overs," said Walter Walter. "You've had two weeks to practice both techniques, standing and sitting."

"Sitting, huh? Franny and Walter *sitting* in a tree, k-i-s-s-i-n-g!" shouted Seymour.

Fleabrain almost bit Seymour but reconsidered.

"Aw, let him stand up and have his do-over," said Franny. "I'll *still* beat him."

Seymour jumped up and swung. His buckeye tapped Franny's, but hers stayed intact.

It was Franny's turn.

Franny faced Seymour with her own steely gaze, raising her buckeye arm. At that moment, Seymour was overcome by a case of hiccups.

"Postpone the challenge on account of hiccups!" yelled Teresa.

"Right! No fair! She'll never hit a jumping buckeye!" hollered Katy, even louder than Teresa, which was saying something.

"Hic!" hiccuped Seymour, his face crumpling into a relieved smile.

"Faker!" shouted B. "He's just stalling."

Seymour shrugged. "Prove—*hic*—it!"

"Postpone the challenge!" said Walter Walter.

"I challenge the postponement!" shouted Franny, raising her arm again. "The tournament continues. No more delays."

To everyone's astonishment, as Seymour's buckeye-on-its-shoelace hiccuped to the left, then hiccuped to the right, Franny's buckeye was waiting at the second hiccup, as if driven to it by an invisible force.

Left. Right. *Crack!*

Seymour's buckeye was down! Franny's buckeye was King-over-25. The rest of the Pack cheered so loudly, a startled Alf scrambled up onto all fours from his afternoon snooze.

Fleabrain was as astonished as everyone else. He'd had nothing at all to do with Franny's win. He hoped she realized that.

Buckeye Amendment #3, Spring 1953
   Hiccups may be grounds for postponement, unless the offense agrees to continue.

Happy for Her

He was happy for her. Oh, he was so happy for her.

He was happy when she pitched that no-hitter on the playground of Colfax School one Sunday, the afternoon another Pack from Northumberland Street decided to let her play, just that once and just for laughs. She surprised them by using her special throw, even more powerful now that her arm was so strong, the ball held in the cleft between her pointing and middle finger. Franny's Whiz Ball. Walter Walter was her runner when Franny was up at bat, and she only struck out once.

He was happy for her when she did a wheelie on Shady Avenue where the street goes downhill at Beacon, and didn't capsize. The Pack gasped as one, in amazement.

And happy for her when she arm-wrestled Walter Walter and won, and even when she arm-wrestled Seymour and Katy and didn't.

But mostly he was happy for her when she wasn't someone special, just one of the Pack. One of the Pack wandering up the street, everyone looking for something to do on a sunny day. Rolling down the paths of Frick Park, needing a push only every now and then. Reading comic books and library books in somebody's living room or backyard, carried up the stairs in a friendship seat. Playing Gin Rummy and Steal the Pile and Old Maid and jacks. Sorting the bottle caps for hours with the other kids in Teresa's basement, according to the caps' rarity, condition, and duplication. Racing her wheelchair down the street in a game of tag, yelling "Safe!" when she touched a tree. And pretending not to hear her parents calling her inside, when the sunset shadows stretched along the sidewalks.

She had a good arm and a good eye and a good heart and, of course, a good head—all the things she'd had Before. The difference was that now she couldn't walk. She didn't even like to try. She hated the kind of walking they wanted her to do, even though she practiced every now and then.

Lean on left foot. Swing right hip out. Step with right foot.

Lean on right foot. Swing left hip out. Step with left foot.

She preferred her wheelchair.

"I wear glasses to help me see," she told her parents. "My wheelchair helps me move. I'm not a pedestrian anymore. Sure, it's a tight squeeze through some doorways, but most of the time this chair is my noble steed. Or my chariot, its golden wheels embedded with precious jewels! And no more hot towels or stretching exercises, please. They're not helping me anymore."

Fleabrain was happy for her, even though her parents protested. But he could see that their eyes were happy for their daughter, too. One of the Pack again, in her wheelchair.

Happy for her.

Happy as the day was long.

And the day was long whenever Francine left the house. Soon it would be longer, for Fleabrain learned something that made his innards quiver.

"I see no reason why your bright daughter can't finish the school year in the classroom with her friends. I'm going to recommend that she does," he heard Mrs. Nelson say to Franny's parents. "The authorities already know she's not contagious, and she is as 'independently mobile' as she needs to be. Keeping her out of Creswell is plain old discrimination, in my opinion."

Franny would be gone all the livelong day, where Alf and, *ipso facto*, he, Fleabrain, couldn't reach her.

Was mich nicht umbringt, macht mich stärker.

What doesn't destroy me, makes me stronger. He wasn't at all sure he believed that anymore. Nietzsche didn't know everything!

He, Fleabrain, certainly wasn't stronger. His formerly burnished shell was as dull as an old penny from the early nineteen-forties. He had no appetite, despite Alf's splendid generosity. Dark dreams penetrated his sleep. His legs were weak and shivery, and his jumping wasn't as powerful as it used to be. What was the point, if there was no joy for which to leap? Life had no meaning if he and Francine couldn't be friends.

During his saddest hours, he listlessly dragged himself to the night table beside her bed. There, he would leaf through *Charlotte's Web*, examining its humorous illustrations, an attempt to feel closer to his Francine, however indirectly. This comforted him greatly. One day, by accident, and with nothing better to do, he began rereading the book in earnest. He'd never, ever reread a book three times, even his beloved *Paramoigraphy*!

Oh, how he tittered and guffawed! Tears came to the tiny eye on each side of his head. He clapped his tarsi with delight throughout his reading. The simple beauty, the fun, the heart of it! A book for any age, for any species, including fleas who thought they knew everything. And yet he was at a loss to explain why the book made him feel so strongly at this, his third, reading. He couldn't seem to analyze its power in a manner befitting his huge brainpower.

Dearest Francine,
I love Charlotte's Web.
Therefore, as your friend, I would be happy
if you read it,
but, of course, you already have.
Yours,
FB

P.S. I couldn't help noticing that you haven't answered any of my previous notes. You have other things to do, of course. I am happy for you.

Happy for her. Happy as the day was long.
But he was brokenhearted for himself.

What Fleabrain Knew
but Wished He Didn't

Music floated up and through Alf's tail hairs, haunting and piercing, like the sharpening of knives. Or chalk across a blackboard. Or the keening of wild creatures not of this planet. Scores, hundreds, perhaps thousands of the tiny, high-pitched voices harmonized together, louder than ever.

"Fleabrain, you are sum-moned. Fleabrain, you are sum-moned. Fleabrain, you are sum-moned."

Fleabrain was terrified. If he wore boots on his tarsi, he'd be shivering in them.

"Alf?" Fleabrain whispered into the dark, his voice quaking.

"Huh?" Alf had been dreaming about lamb bones. "What's wrong?"

"Do you hear it?"

"Hear what?" asked Alf. He yawned and flicked his tail and, thus, Fleabrain, back and forth.

"Whoa!" said Fleabrain, hanging on to Alf's hair. "You're pretty vigorous for two in the morning!"

"Sorry. I feel an odd, tingling sensation in my tail. What's happening back there?"

"Nothing out of the ordinary," said Fleabrain. "Having a bit of supper, that's all. But, Alf, do you hear the singing?"

Fleabrain, you are sum-moned.
Fleabrain, you are sum-moned.
Fleabrain, you are sum-moned.

The choristers had now chosen a higher key, relentless and insistent.

"Did you say you were singing, Fleabrain? I didn't know you could sing," said Alf.

"Yes, of course I can sing," said Fleabrain waspishly. "I'm a magnificent tenor, as fine as our famous American tenor Mario Lanza, born January 31, 1921. Oh, how I wish I had time to regale you with *'E lucevan le stelle'* from the opera *Tosca*, by the Italian composer Giacomo Puccini, born December 22, 1858, died November 29, 1924! It's the aria the imprisoned artist Cavaradossi sings while awaiting execution, entirely appropriate to the present situation. But that's not me singing now. Alf, can't you hear the choir? It's mighty loud this time."

Alf cocked an ear. "Nope."

"What's wrong with you? You're a dog. Hearing's supposed to be your major talent, second only to smelling! Don't you hear it?"

Alf tried again. "No choir. Sorry."

Fleabrain, you are sum-moned.
Fleabrain, you are sum-moned.
Fleabrain, you are sum-moned.

Of course Alf couldn't process the sound! Alf had never heard the singing because the sound had always been too small for even a dog's ears to process, *small* being the operative word here. And the smaller the sound, the greater the importance.

The greater the power.

Fleabrain, you are sum-moned.
Fleabrain, you are sum-moned.
Fleabrain, you are sum-moned.

The choir was making no attempt to harmonize or sing on key now. Foreboding and discordant, the command filled Fleabrain's "ears."

"OK, OK, I'm on my way!" shouted Fleabrain. He might as well face the music. He would try, in these last, terrifying moments, to be brave, if he could.

Alf turned his head. "Where are you going at this hour?" he asked.

"Your guess is as good as mine," said Fleabrain.

He rubbed himself all over with FB Saliva #3, a solution perfected to make the tiny even tinier. His jaws clattered with dread.

Fleabrain, you are sum-moned.
Fleabrain, you are sum-moned.
Fleabrain, you are sum-moned.

"Good-bye, dear world!" he whispered. "Good-bye, books! Good-bye, Alf, dear friend! Good-bye, my dearest, dearest Francine!"

He felt the squeezing deep down in his "gut." He could hardly breathe. He smelled the popcorn and the firecrackers. He heard a rushing sound like trees swaying and shaking in a storm, as he clutched his favorite tail hair, now as wide as a redwood tree.

"Fleabrain, you are sum-moned. Fleabrain, you are sum-moned. Fleabrain, you are sum-moned," sang the choir, louder and closer now.

"You want me smaller still?" gasped Fleabrain. He took another FB Saliva #3 bath, gamely rubbing it all over his body. "Now what?"

He felt himself hurtling downward, then sideways, then up, then down again. The process seemed to take forever, but his reliable instincts told him a mere three seconds had gone by. His favorite Alf hair was no longer a hair or even a tree but a dull, flat surface stretching endlessly toward infinity.

And then he became aware of them, thousands of them, sitting in rows all around him. They were waiting for the show to begin, as if they were patrons of the Manor Theater on Murray Avenue, except that the theater seemed as big as a stadium.

On closer inspection, Fleabrain realized they weren't all sitting. Some lounged on their sides; others bobbed up and down; some attached themselves to others and hogged a whole row. Others continuously morphed and divided into exact replicas of themselves.

Fleabrain recognized a few of them from illustrations in *The Invisible World*, a biology book in the Katzenback bookcase: the pancake-shaped skin cells; the snaky nerve cells with their enthusiastic dendrites; the blood cells, round like sucking candy; a random buglike bacterium. He'd never thought he'd see them for himself, these creatures of another world. Except the world was Alf, or Alf's tail, to be precise. Wonders of the microworld, which he certainly would have appreciated under different circumstances.

"Fleabrain!" the group intoned, the sound large and commanding.

"Yes?" Fleabrain whispered.

"You have been summoned!"

"I'm aware of that," replied Fleabrain dryly.

They all burst into an otherworldly, screeching laughter, with some applause.

"Yes, I'm sure you are," a few skin and muscle cells shouted in unison.

"Who or What has summoned me?"

"You have been summoned by the Commanders of All Nuclei!" cried the giant group, once again in unison. "And we have been named the Great and Powerful and Majestic Council of the Small. For today, anyway."

"Who are the Commanders of All Nuclei?" Fleabrain asked, and the crowd burst into laughter once again.

"Oh, my, what a question!" sang a blood cell, floating to the front of the stadium as the apparently designated "spokescell." "All right, enough frivolity, everyone. 'They' are the deepest level beneath us, in the Great Beyond Below. The Life Force, the Very Nature of Things, even smaller and more powerful than we. 'They' will be monitoring and guiding our discussion as it transpires. 'They' have asked us to pronounce judgment after evaluating the situation."

"What situation?" Fleabrain asked.

The group roared with laughter once again. It was not unpleasant, Fleabrain decided, finding himself to be so effortlessly witty.

"Quiet, quiet!" shouted a furious bacterium. "Let's be serious! The situation of *you*, Fleabrain, you little mutation. What you are, what you've been, what you've done, and whether you will be or do whatever, ever again!"

"Oh," said Fleabrain.

"Come on, it's not as bad as that!" yelled a group of tightly coiled cells from the higher-up seats.

"Oh, yeah?" responded the bacterium, to the applause of a few of his cronies.

"Now, now," admonished the blood cell, "let us proceed, using proper decorum and procedure, one flaw at a time."

And so the discussion began.

Fleabrain had been arrogant, sometimes selfish, often envious.

He had bragged, flaunting his great knowledge.

He was not a good listener.

He had lied and shammed.

His ancestors had helped carry and spread disease. (This last point was mightily argued down by the majority for its prejudice. Fleabrain was but one lone flea, not to be held responsible for the past actions of others.)

Most of the arguments were not a surprise to Fleabrain. He shivered in humiliation and with much regret.

At this point, a Y-shaped creature bounced to the front of the stadium. "May I have the floor? We are not being entirely fair here." She extended her long arms sympathetically toward Fleabrain.

"Proceed, Aunty Boddy," said the spokecell.

"I have vital work to do in the bloodstream, fighting off infections, but I came to this meeting to ensure that the Council consider the flea's good qualities," she said.

"Let us all enumerate them!" shouted the audience.

The crowd called out a few of Fleabrain's positives:

He was an entertaining conversationalist.

He was appreciative of and kind to his host.

He was well-bred and well-read.

He was full of fun.

He was flawed, but he meant no harm.

And always, a ceaseless advocate for the power of the small.

Then, suddenly, from the Great Beyond Below, came a rushing, whispery monotone, a million voices from everywhere, speaking as a group, phrases tumbling one after another like leaves on a windy day. Fleabrain presumed these were the Commanders of All Nuclei, weighing in. The stadium immediately fell silent.

and

he has loved

yes, he has loved

yes

"Right!" shouted Fleabrain, almost weeping with gratitude. He waved a tibia defiantly. "I have loved! Doesn't that count for a lot?" His pumping mechanism soared with hope.

Yes, he had loved, the members of the Council agreed.

"But selfishly," said a nerve cell, pointing an accusing finger—like dendrite, "with not a shred of agape!"

"No agape! No agape! No agape!" the bacteria jeered, and to Fleabrain's dismay, a few in the crowd picked up the chant. "No agape! No agape! No agape!"

Fleabrain lay prostrate before them all, unable to move, paralyzed by shame.

It was true. For once in his life Fleabrain wished he didn't know what he knew. But he knew very well what *agape* meant in this context. Francine had known, too. Fleabrain hadn't had any agape, or very much at all, where Francine was concerned.

Agape. From the Greek: /ægəpiː/[1] or /əgaːper/; Classical Greek: ἀγάπη, agápē; Modern Greek: αγάπη IPA: [aˈɣapi]

Selfless love.

He had loved Franny mostly to feel less lonely, wanting her all to himself. He hadn't been entirely considerate of Francine's need to grow, to discover Wonders on her own.

Fleabrain sobbed. His instincts told him what he had to do, in order to truly love his Francine. He knew, but, oh, how he wished he didn't! How he wished for the bliss of ignorance!

And now, proclaimed the Commanders of All Nuclei,

council do
do
do
your duty

Fleabrain shivered uncontrollably while the vast crowd buzzed quietly, discussing and voting upon the situation; i.e., himself.

Finally the portly blood cell announced, "We are ready to deliver our verdict, Fleabrain. Which do you want first, the good news or the bad news?"

"The bad news," he whispered. Anyway, he already knew what it was.

"The bad news," continued the spokescell, "is the end of your personal relationship with Franny. For her own good."

"Does it really have to be?" cried Fleabrain, knowing full well that it did. His powerful instincts had been correct.

yes
yes
yes

hissed the Commanders of All Nuclei, but not unkindly.

"I can't let her go," whispered Fleabrain. His heart mechanism felt as if it was breaking into a million tiny shards.

you can
you can

"She doesn't want to talk to me again, anyway," said Fleabrain. "She doesn't need me anymore."

wrong
as you will see
you will see

The spokescell continued. "You must say good-bye to Franny (and please call her Franny, not Francine, as does everyone else in her world) with just three written words. You have been entirely too verbose and abstruse in your dealings with her."

"Three words?" Fleabrain was aghast at the group's rigidity, not to mention its lack of literary sensibility. What could be said in a mere three words?

"Just three," continued the spokescell, "in the style of Charlotte. She was a brilliant spinner of few words, and a genius at distilling friendship down to its most important elements."

"Does all this mean I will never see Franny again?" asked Fleabrain.

The audience erupted into laughter, which went on and on for several minutes. Just as the laughter died down to a trickle, a snort or a giggle would start it all up again.

Finally the blood cell pulled herself together. "My dear flea. You must never, never, never say *never*!" And the crowd began laughing all over again.

Silence, all

we bring
we bring
the good news, now
now

spoke the Commanders of All Nuclei.

A sudden hush fell over the multitudes, a silence so deep and powerful, Fleabrain could hardly breathe.

Fleabrain, the Commanders continued,
Franny must stay in her world, not yours
we demand you let her go
go
go
having faith that you will do so
but we promise
promise
promise
you will remember your friendship forever
as will she
and your memories will assuage your loneliness
and inspire your writing
and bring happiness to you both
and you yourself will be remembered as
one of the
truest friends in history and fiction
who arrives when he is needed

and takes his leave when he is not
and is thus now deemed
deemed
deemed
SOME FLEA.

The words of the Commanders of All Nuclei enveloped Fleabrain like a warm, downy coverlet. He felt peaceful and sated and much larger somehow, as if he'd just supped on a blood feast after a long, hard day.

He, a little orphan flea, usually so reviled, felt beloved.

"SOME FLEA! SOME FLEA!" intoned the crowd of microscopic beings before him.

The blood spokescell stepped forward. "Of course, you will receive no plaque!" The audience tittered at the pun. "But know that we are all aware of your specialness. Let's give him a big hand, folks."

The crowd applauded, using their various tendrils and extensions. Some of them bumped one another in a joyous, celebratory way. Others divided into other congratulatory cells, who joined the acclamation, as well.

"Do you have a speech to make, sir?" asked the blood cell.

Fleabrain shook his head, even though he understood that some sort of literate, gracious statement was often required on such an occasion. "Thank you, but I'm afraid words fail me at the moment" was all he could mumble in a choked-up voice. For what could one say when one was both happy and miserable at the same time?

Very well, Fleabrain
once you were merely clever
now you are wise
and now
now
this meeting is

The voices of the Commanders of All Nuclei faded slowly into the Great Beyond Below.

adjourned.

Fleabrain could already feel the FB Saliva #3 potion beginning to wear off, as his body, if not his spirits, enlarged. A large group of Aunty Boddies swarmed past him, alerted to a possible digestive disturbance in Alf's large intestine. The remaining cells, stimulated by the night's celebrations, decided to participate in a rousing sing-along of popular tunes.

Three little words
Eight little letters

they sang.

I L-O-V-E Y-O-U? Were those to be his three words for Franny? But Fleabrain's instincts told him the cells were taunting him, challenging him to think beyond the obvious.

An Envelope Like Many Others

I t was a rainy day, but it wasn't dreary.

The rain fell in torrents, splashing against Franny's slightly open window and drizzling onto the sill. There was nothing much to see—cars slowly inching by, an occasional colorful umbrella, a blurred figure huddled beneath it.

Franny loved the fragrance of a rainy day, the sidewalk's wet concrete, the yard's rosebush, more alive than ever. She could be a weather girl on KDKA, just by announcing the smells and sounds from her own bedroom window! Smells and sounds gave so much information.

October. The crackle of burning leaves, the air crisp but not cold, with an applelike smell. Fifty-five degrees.

February. Hushed crunch of tires on snowy streets, the odor of a cigarette burning in the cold, clear air. Twenty degrees.

May. Birds, of course. Warm breeze, smelling of gasoline. People laughing. Over sixty degrees.

She could be a weather girl, that's how well she knew the world from her bedroom window on Shady Avenue. She didn't even need to look. She didn't even need to go outside. She could smell, hear, and imagine it all. And soon she wouldn't need to imagine it anymore! She would be out there herself, in all types of weather.

She wouldn't have to imagine her school desk anymore, either, with its scrawled-on surface. *Rob Loves Carol. U.S.A. Forever.* Her fifth-grade desk would have different scrawls, of course. And on the wall, a portrait of the new president, Dwight D. Eisenhower, the flag in the corner of the room, the tall windows that needed a long pole to open them, and the dancing cursive letters above the blackboard. The scraping chairs and clanging bells and shouts and chatter of her friends. She wouldn't have to imagine or remember anymore. She would be there, right there, with everyone else!

Back in school. Back in school.

And she wouldn't have to think about her bedroom much, the little bedroom she knew so well, every inch memorized from ceiling to floor and wall to wall. The "Cheer up!" dracaena plant. The braided rug. Her matching oak furniture, every scratch and water stain. The little bookcase with her favorite books.

Alf.

Dear, dear Fleabrain.

No, she wouldn't have to think about her bedroom. All she'd have to do was spend time in it after school, at night, and, every now and then, on weekends and rainy days.

Like a regular girl.

If it was raining, her parents could drive her to school. If the weather was fine, Katy and Walter Walter would be with her as she rolled her wheelchair. They'd make that special seat for her, hands over wrists, to carry her up the stairs at school, then go down again to fetch her chair. Such good friends! She would wear her braces and, yes, her clodhopper shoes. And even walk her stilted walk for very short distances.

But only if she had to.

And sometimes, she just knew, she and her wheelchair would pop a wheelie in the halls!

Back in school. Back in school.

Franny pushed herself to her desk to look over the mimeo-graphed sheet Mrs. Nelson had given her to prepare for the spring General Info Bee.

What is the second longest river in the world?
In what country were the first ancient Olympics held?
Where is Stonehenge?
What are the three branches of American government?
What percentage of Earth is made up of water?

Easy! Easy-peasy!

Even if she missed some answers, who cared, really? Everyone else would be missing some, too.

She heard a soft knock at her bedroom door.

"It's all right, Mom," said Franny. "Come on in."

Her mother came into the room, carrying the day's mail and a chicken sandwich for Franny. She sat down on Franny's bed, leafing through the letters and bills.

Mrs. Katzenback opened a cream-colored envelope and drew out a single sheet of matching stationery. "No," she said.

"What is it, Mom?" asked Franny, her mouth full of sandwich. "A big bill?"

It was an envelope like many others, official and boring-looking.

"Franny." The envelope fell from her mother's hand and fluttered to the floor. "Franny," she repeated, reaching out to hold her daughter close.

Franny looked down at the cream-colored stationery in her mother's hand. She recognized Creswell School's letterhead, an old-fashioned purple crest with a cheerful green ribbon of Latin words inside of it. *Crescente luce.* That meant "light ever increasing," she'd been told back in second grade. Franny used to think that *crescente luce* had to do with the day getting brighter toward morning recess and lunch. But everybody knew that Pittsburgh skies, compared to other skies, got much sootier as the day went on!

Understanding the phrase's true meaning was beyond the capabilities of second-grade Franny.

Fifth-grade Franny now understood that *crescente luce* meant the increase of wisdom. That same purple crest with its ribbon of Latin words had always been stamped at the top of Franny's report cards, which were sprinkled all over with A's and the very occasional B. To Franny, the crest meant happiness, pride, and wisdom. All the happy, proud wisdom of the whole wide world, ever increasing, and all of it Franny's for the taking.

But not this time.

Dear Mr. and Mrs. Katzenback,

It has come to my attention that Mrs. Penelope Nelson has invited your daughter, Francine Katzenback, a polio victim, to return to her classroom before our school closes its doors for the summer break. Mrs. Nelson praises your daughter's ability to keep up with the rest of her classmates with regard to her studies. I am sure you are very proud of her.

Be that as it may, I must apologize for Mrs. Nelson, who does not understand the situation, due to her relative inexperience as a teacher. I'm afraid the school cannot accommodate your daughter. No wheelchair is allowed on the school property, especially considering the many stairs inside and uneven walkways outdoors. In addition, the presence of a wheelchair and other accoutrements of Francine's handicap would be a distraction to the other students, a hardship for your daughter, and a liability for the school.

We are fortunate to have the excellent Memorial Home for Crippled Children right here in Squirrel Hill, a much better choice for Francine next year. There, she will find others in similar circumstances. There, her wheelchair would not be an obstacle. I would urge you to investigate that institution as best befitting your daughter's needs.

Sincerely,

A . L. Woolcott

Principal, Creswell School

No Wheelchair

NO WHEELchair
NO wheelCHAIR
The words in the letter were magnified by Franny's tears. When the tears splashed on top of the principal's splendid handwriting, the words swam in a crooked, taunting line down the page.

> NO
>
>   WHEEL
>
>   CHAIR

And even when her mother gently took the letter and hid it in the pocket of her dress, Franny could still hear them in her mind: *No Wheelchair* . . .

Later, her parents brought supper to her bedroom. Her father carried the plate of food and a tall glass of milk. Her mother placed a wooden tray with fold-out legs across Franny's knees as she sat on Franny's bed.

Macaroni and stewed tomatoes, a sprightly sprig of parsley on the side to make it look fancy.

"I'm not sick," said Franny.

"Of course you're not," said her father. "But you should eat."

"I'm too unhappy to eat," she said. She wondered if she'd ever feel like eating again. "I don't want to go to the Memorial Home for Crippled Children, Mama."

Usually she called her mother Mom. But "Mama" just popped out.

"It's a nice school, Franny," said her mother. "And it's time for you to leave your room."

The Home *was* nice, Franny remembered. She used to speed by it on her bike. It was on Shady Avenue, but in a fancier part of the neighborhood, right near the Tree of Life Synagogue. The school building wasn't very tall; there weren't a lot of stairs to worry about. There were flowers in front, and the walkways were smooth. In the play area she sometimes saw children playing together in wheelchairs or on crutches, many wearing leg braces.

"I don't understand why they need a whole separate building just for kids in wheelchairs," she said. "Hey, I also wear glasses! Why don't they have a Home for Nearsighted Children?"

Her father smoothed the pillowcase behind her head. "You know it's a bit more complicated than that, honey," he said.

"I just wish they would give me more time to practice my walking. I promise, I'll practice every single minute."

Her parents were holding hands. They looked at one another. Franny could tell they were trying as hard as they could not to cry, to help Franny look at the bright side of things. That was a parent's job. And Franny loved them very much for trying to do something so hard. Something impossible.

As impossible as her ever walking again, even if she stole all the days' marches from the sun, just as the writer James Joyce described, and practiced walking forever and ever. She knew that now.

"Franny, come listen to the radio with us in the kitchen. *The Charlie McCarthy Show* is on," said her mother.

"I really don't feel like laughing," said Franny.

"Well, you can't just stay holed up in your room," said her father.

"Yes, I can," Franny said. "That's what the poet Emily Dickinson did."

Min came to sit on Franny's bed later that evening. "Oh, Franny," she said. She didn't tell Franny to eat or leave her room or stop crying, and, anyway, she was crying herself. Alf licked Min's face. Franny loved Min for being Min.

The ballerina leaped strenuously at 9:37 P.M., but even she seemed tired of the struggle. Franny, slipping to the floor, dragged herself to her closet across the room to dig out her journal.

Dear, dear Fleabrain,
I miss you very much. We have so many more Wonders to explore. Please come back.
Love always,
Franny

Lying on the braided rug, Alf stirred.

"Fleabrain?" Franny whispered. She pulled herself to the night table and found the tiny leftover fragment of Sparky's Finest she kept in a drawer. Alf came to her, and she held the glass to her eye as she carefully combed through the dog's tail with her other hand. She turned her head to search the room. Splinters of moonlight. A blur of gray shadow.

But no Fleabrain.

"Fleabrain, can you hear me?" Franny asked. "Where are you? Fleabrain, what should I do?"

Three Little Words

Of course he could hear her!

"I can hear the beating of your heart and every single breath you breathe!" Fleabrain wanted to shout as he watched Franny from Alf's hairy flank.

But he couldn't say that to her. Those words were embarrassingly maudlin and flowery, not to mention more than three, his allowable quota.

That night Fleabrain labored at discovering the three perfect words to help his dear, dear Francine. Shakespeare, Rumi, Neruda, Kafka, Dickinson, Hughes, the esteemed Howell—no great writer in all of history ever labored harder at his or her creative task.

Certainly a mere three words should be easy to compose.

He industriously filled one and one-half pages of Franny's journal.

I love you.
~~Some girl, Franny.~~

~~Do not worry.~~
~~Count to ten.~~
~~Roses are red.~~
~~Chin up, Franny.~~
~~Be proud, Franny.~~
~~You are terrific.~~
~~Never fear, Franny.~~
~~Always hope, Franny.~~
~~Fleabrain loves Franny.~~
~~Fleabrain cherishes Franny~~
~~Hooray for you.~~
~~Salutes to you.~~
~~You will prevail.~~
~~You will succeed.~~
~~Friends forever, Franny.~~
~~Comrades forever, Franny.~~
~~Amigos forever, Franny.~~
~~Hello, I'm here.~~
~~Fleabrain is here.~~
~~Really, I'm here.~~

None of those measly, three-word sentences would truly help Franny, Fleabrain knew. He was blocked, hopelessly and frighteningly stymied, despite his huge, incomparable brainpower.

Frustrated, Fleabrain lay curled on the floor in a "fetal" position. One tiny eye stared at the ceiling, willing his IQ to help him create. He could hear Franny crying in her bed, unable to sleep. Bug it! It was just too much. Who cared about the threats and demands of the Commanders of All Nuclei! Posh on the Great and Powerful and Majestic Council of the Small! He would write Franny an ode of one thousand verses proclaiming his love, inviting her to join him in a Wonder-filled life, forever and ever.

No. That wasn't what Franny needed.

And then Fleabrain saw it.

High up in its usual corner, lit by moonlight, was the small web of the angry brown spider. A lopsided, accidental *Z* had been spun smack-dab in the web's center.

Of course, it meant nothing, nothing at all. But with no other available source of inspiration, in his terrible frustration and desperation, Fleabrain decided to give it his creative all, one more time. He began to brainstorm using that *Z*.

~~You have zeal~~
~~You are my zenith.~~
~~I am Zorro.~~
~~Zinc melts 419.5 C.~~
~~My zinnia, Franny.~~

Oh. Wait.

He, Fleabrain, was not the one to help Franny this time, after all. It would be someone else who loved her. Someone from her own world.

Ask your Zadie, Fleabrain wrote.

No need to cross anything out. Fleabrain's instincts told him that those three words were perfect.

Zadie's TOTU

Zadie Ben was singing a lullaby.

Franny had telephoned him the evening before. She'd told him she missed him. Would he have an answer? she'd wondered to herself. Trouble was, she wasn't even sure what her question would be.

And there he was in her bedroom the next morning, singing a lullaby. There were several things wrong with that.

First of all, lullabies were for evening. And Zadie Ben usually sang after Friday-night supper, not Sunday breakfast.

Second of all, lullabies were for sleeping. She knew that Zadie Ben wanted her to wake up, not sleep. Everybody wanted her to do that. Get out of bed, get dressed, greet the morning sun, and smile, smile, smile. Like an uncomplaining poster child.

Third of all, Franny didn't understand the lullaby. The words of the song were in Yiddish. That had never bothered her before, during all the hundreds of times she'd heard it. The tune itself was as familiar as her bathrobe, so familiar, she'd hardly realized there were words along with it. Zadie Ben said he'd learned the song at his mother's knee, and his mother had learned it at her mother's knee, who'd learned it at *her* mother's knee. Franny imagined a dizzying line of plump knees and warm laps going way, way back in time. Everyone in that line knew what the song meant, except her.

He was sitting in her desk chair, which he'd dragged close to her bed. His eyes were closed, and he held his worn, slipperlike shoes in his lap. He had taken them off to be comfortable because he'd been sitting there for a long time. Zadie Ben smelled like pancakes and tea, and Franny realized she was hungry. She reached for his hand.

Zadie Ben's eyes opened slowly, as if he'd been singing in his sleep. But his cheeks were pink and his eyebrows wriggling, and Franny loved him so much, she wished he could live forever.

"What's that song about, anyway?" she asked.

And so he told her.

The song was an old, old story set to music by someone who preferred to sing. Before the universe was created, the song went, God filled clay vessels with the sparks of light necessary to make an absolutely perfect world.

"Of course, that made for some pretty powerful ingredients," said Zadie Ben. "The pressure was enormous! KABOOM!"

He sang the song again, in English this time.

The vessels of light shattered,
Shards scattered,
Piercing the sparks,
Hiding the sparks,

Those precious sparks!
Then tumbling, tumbling down.

"Can you imagine the giant explosion?" he asked her. "Yes," Franny whispered. She'd seen the newsreels of the bomb bursting over Hiroshima. It was easy to imagine the noise and the stink and the heat, as the vessels of light shattered into shards. She imagined all the broken pieces swirling about the firmament, piercing and trapping the beautiful light, then the shards tumbling down to Earth. It must have been beautiful and terrifying, all at once, and thank goodness no one had been there to experience it.

"And that was that," said Zadie Ben. "The world ended up, as everyone knows, not-so-perfect. We've been trying to free the light from those broken shards ever since."

"Someone from long ago had a wonderful imagination," Franny said.

Zadie Ben rubbed his chin thoughtfully. There was a sugarlike sprinkling of white bristles on his face. He'd arrived very early that morning and needed a shave. "You're right; it may not have happened exactly like that," he said, "but the song and its story still tell the truth. The important thing to know is that it's the world that needs to be repaired, not you, *feygeleh*. So leave your bedroom and help us fix it."

"Me?" Franny pulled herself up to a sitting position. "How can I fix it?"

Zadie Ben leaned over to kiss her cheek. The white bristles above his mouth tickled. "You'll figure it out," he said.

"Well, now she knows," said Fleabrain.

Fleabrain and the brown spider were both lying companionably on the window ledge several days later, warmed by a sun ray.

"Yes, now she knows," echoed the spider.

"Franny will be very busy, freeing the light from her world's broken shards," said Fleabrain. Tears filled his tiny eyes. He would miss her very much.

"By the way, I've been meaning to tell you," said the spider. "That *Z* in my web wasn't accidental. I spun it on purpose."

"The thought crossed my mind," said Fleabrain. "Thanks for the tip."

"I did it for Franny. She and her clarinet saved my life, that day you were both cavorting inside my web."

"I remember, I remember," said Fleabrain. "Don't rub it in. No hard feelings?"

"Not at all," said the spider. "All's well that ends well, as the Bard would say."

Fleabrain clapped several tarsi. "Shakespeare! You're a reader!"

"I've been known to peruse a bit, when time allows me to leave the web."

"I just realized we haven't been formally introduced. I'm Fleabrain, *Ctenocephalides canis.*"

"Chuck, here. *Parasteatoda tepidariorum.*"

Fleabrain leaped seven inches into the air. "You're kidding!" he shouted. "Your name is *Chuck*? Short for Charles?"

The spider's multiple eyes looked hurt. "Charles is my given name, yes. What's the matter? You have a problem with it?"

"No problem at all, actually. It's a perfectly distinguished name. In fact, may I call you Charles?"

"I would love that. No one has ever called me Charles, except my dear, departed mom."

"Charles, my good friend," said Fleabrain. "I'd like to share some information with you, but please keep it between you and me. Franny plans to begin repairing the world very soon. OK, not exactly the whole world. Just her little part of it."

"And her plan is . . . ?"

"You'll see, you'll see," said Fleabrain.

The ballerina danced away the minutes of the afternoon. With each minute, Fleabrain's happiness grew, as he marveled at the miracle of a spider and a flea, perched side by side on one beam of light. Another Truth of the Universe, he realized. Kindred Spirits were everywhere!

"Say, Charles, have you read Howell's *Paramoigraphy*?" Fleabrain asked.

"Can't say that I have."

"Charles, I think you'll love it."

A Statement

Nicholson Street was steep, but Franny said she preferred that route, and Min and Milt helped her from behind.

The birds of dawn were twittering, her heart was beating, and Alf was panting as he trudged beside her wheelchair. Somewhere on Alf's tail, Fleabrain was cheering. From Franny's perspective, things were quite noisy. From Min and Milt's perspective, Franny guessed, it was a quiet morning, with a silvery sky and a splash of sunrise. Very romantic.

"Are you OK, kiddo?" Milt asked.

"I'm perfect, *langer loksh*," Franny said.

Milt had arrived at the Katzenback home at 6:00 A.M. Franny was ready, dressed, and waiting in her chair. She was wearing her braces and her clodhopper shoes. Milt picked her up and carried her, and Min pushed the wheelchair, quietly and swiftly, out the front door.

Soon they were quickly crossing the boulevard, then moving more slowly along the wooded path, the morning sun slanting through the trees.

"Mom and Dad will be reading my note soon," Min said. "I taped it on Dad's shaving mirror."

"They'll be angry," said Franny. "Worried, too." That was the only flaw in her plan.

"Oh, phooey!" said Min. "This is important. I told them everything would be fine, and to meet us there at eight. They'll be there."

Oh, phooey?

Who was this spunky, angry Min, flyaway hair in her eyes, her cheeks as pink as cotton candy? Where had Saint Min gone? Franny wondered at the change in her sister, ever since that awful letter from the school had arrived. Or did it have something to do with falling in love? Or maybe this more spirited Min had been secretly hiding all along, waiting for an important reason to show up.

And here was one reason. As they entered Lightning's stall, he bent his head way down to nuzzle Franny's neck, as always. She kissed his velvet nose, then put both arms around his neck to whisper the secret of their next adventure into his ear.

"I'll be right back," said Milt. He ran into the stables' office and emerged with a picnic hamper. "Before we go, breakfast for all of us."

Milt spread a blue-checked tablecloth on a picnic table in front of the stables.

Bagels, cream cheese, melon, and apples. Blueberry pie and eleven dog biscuits. It was probably the best breakfast of all of their lives.

After breakfast, Franny fed Lightning an apple, then watched Milt brush him until his rich brown hide gleamed like a buckeye. He checked Lightning's tail for stickers and hay and cleaned his feet with a pick.

"Next time you'll help me," Milt said to Franny.

"Are you going to get into trouble for all of this?" Franny asked.

"Maybe," Milt said. "Maybe not. Lightning's my aunt's horse." Milt's dark eyes crinkled when he smiled. Franny understood why Min loved him.

Milt tacked up Lightning and walked him around the stables a few times to warm his muscles.

"Hey, Milt, it's getting late," said Min. "It's time."

"Ready, Franny?" asked Milt.

"Ready," said Franny.

Ready.

Milt picked her up, and he and Min carefully helped Franny straddle the horse's saddle and put her feet into the stirrups. Franny held the reins while her sister stood beside her, Min's hand on Franny's leg.

"Walk on, old fellow. You won't be traveling very far," said Milt. He held a rope attached to Lightning's halter.

Lightning started forward slowly, guided by Milt, Alf following the horse.

"You're a natural, kiddo!" said Milt.

Franny sat tall. She'd done this before. "Thank you," she said.

The procession turned down English Lane, then onto the sidewalk of Beechwood Boulevard, which was now alive with cars and people. Horns honked, and people gawked at the girl on her horse on the sidewalks of Squirrel Hill. Milt held up his hand to stop the traffic as they crossed the boulevard at the corner. Only one more block to go.

There were so many things in the world to repair, Franny knew. But there were so many things that didn't need repairing at all.

The sun on her back, like a warm cloak.

Min's smile that morning.

Alf.

Lightning, her noble champion, his true speed and aerial power known only to a few.

Her love for her family and her friends.

Charlotte's Web.

Her love for Fleabrain, always and forever.

They had reached the school. Walter Walter and Katy had told the rest of the Pack who told everyone else, and now there was a respectful silence as Franny and Lightning trotted into the school yard. Every kid had imagined themselves sitting upon that beautiful old racehorse. No one would ever forget Franny's ride.

Franny saw her parents, with tenuous smiles and concerned frowns, just as Min had predicted. But she hadn't expected to see the young man with a camera.

"Jimmy Regis, here," he said, wearing a press badge and a smile. "Special Correspondent to the *Pittsburgh Rag*. Do you have a statement to make, miss?"

"A statement? Well, yes, I do," said Franny. "My name is Francine Babette Katzenback. I'm in fifth grade, and I want to go to school with my friends. I'm not allowed to come in my wheelchair, so I came on a horse. They may not let me stay at Creswell, but here I am today."

"May I?" Jimmy asked, holding up his camera. Franny nodded, and a bulb flashed.

Min and Milt helped her down, and Franny walked across the yard, holding on to Min's arm. Lean on left foot. Swing right hip out. Step with right foot. Lean on right foot. Swing left hip out. Step with left foot.

She could see Mrs. Nelson, waving from a second-floor window. Franny could tell she was singing. At the Girls' Entrance, Katy and Teresa made a friendship seat, hands over wrists, stronger than rope. Franny put her arms around the girls' shoulders and pulled herself up, and they climbed the stairs to their classroom.

Rag

un...
night, w...
morrow,
high 68. We...

Thursday, May 28, 1953

SMALL STEPS FOR CHANGE BY SMALL RIDER

by Jimmy Regis, Special Correspondent

An anonymous citizen tipped this reporter that the Gateway Angel would be arriving at Squirrel Hill's Creswell School yesterday at 8:00 a.m. sharp.

Instead, I met student Francine B. Katzenback, who had entered the school yard astride a magnificent old racehorse, Lightning, in order to make an equally magnificent statement for equality and inclusion.

Francine (Franny to her friends), stricken by polio last summer, is ready and able to return to school, but was told she could not be accommodated. Her presence at school proved otherwise.

AUTHOR'S NOTE

Charlotte's Web, written by E. B. White and illustrated by Garth Williams, was published in October 1952, after the summer of the worst polio outbreak in U.S. history, in which 58,000 cases were recorded.

White's novel is a celebration of life and of a life-saving friendship. Any reader who has ever felt helpless and lonely can identify with the plight of Wilbur, the runt piglet of the litter, doomed to death because of his size. Young polio victims, especially, felt small in the face of their illness, suddenly overwhelmed by a situation in which everyone seemed to know what was best for them, but no one could really help. Perhaps some longed for their own tiny, but mighty, Charlotte. And so I imagined Franny and Fleabrain, the three of us connected by E. B. White's inspiring book.

In the mid-1950s, surveys showed that people in the United States feared polio—also called poliomyelitis or infantile paralysis—more than they feared the atom bomb. The terror they felt was largely the result of their sense of hopelessness in preventing an outbreak, the mysteries of the disease, and the fact that so many children were tragically affected.

Polio has been around since ancient times. The disease is caused by the poliovirus, which enters the intestinal tract through the mouth and may find its way into the bloodstream. It is thought to spread by hand-to-hand contact.

Polio's virulence and incidence increased during the nineteenth and twentieth centuries. Ironically, it was the improvement of sanitation systems that most likely led to polio epidemics. In earlier times, when there were open sewage systems and outdoor latrines, people were exposed to the virus as babies—that is, while they were still partially protected by the maternal antibodies (disease-fighting agents produced by the immune system) in their bloodstream. While they might come down with a mild case of polio, this very early exposure to the poliovirus protected them, because it enabled them to develop their own protective antibodies against future exposure to the disease. Such protection was far less likely to occur in more sanitary times, and older children became vulnerable, since they had not been exposed to the poliovirus as babies.

In the majority of cases during the polio epidemics of the twentieth century, the infected individuals experienced only mild gastrointestinal or respiratory problems. Many did not even realize they were infected (although they could still spread the virus to others). However, for a minority, the virus left the intestinal tract and entered the central nervous system, where it damaged or destroyed motor neurons, resulting in severe muscle weakness or permanent paralysis.

When the virus affected muscles necessary for breathing, patients were in danger of dying; the only way to keep them alive was to place them in an "iron lung," a large, elaborate machine in which they lay immobile, often for days at a time. Many polio patients eventually regained the ability to breathe on their own, to walk, and to function without the aid of an iron lung, braces, crutches, and wheelchairs; others, tragically, did not.

One of those stricken was Franklin Delano Roosevelt, who contracted polio as a young man. After serving as governor of New York,

Roosevelt became president of the United States in 1933. Even though he needed leg braces and a cane in order to stand, he wanted to appear confident and able-bodied to the American public, so his staff discouraged any photographs or films of him in a wheelchair. However, during his presidency, Roosevelt established the National Foundation for Infantile Paralysis to raise money for polio research and financial aid for patients. Because of the huge success of its fund-raising campaigns, in which millions of coins from people of all walks of life, including children, poured into its headquarters from across the nation, the foundation's name was later changed to the March of Dimes.

The desperate race to create a safe and effective vaccine to prevent polio was centered in the United States, funded by the March of Dimes and other foundations. The young Dr. Jonas Salk and his team of dedicated scientists at the University of Pittsburgh, working sixteen-hour days six days a week in the basement and lower floors of the Municipal Hospital for Contagious Diseases, were the first to meet with success. Pittsburgh was, and remains, proud of its association with this team, and Salk did indeed live "somewhere" in Squirrel Hill—although Professor Doctor George Gutman is fictional.

Salk's theory was that a vaccine containing a small amount of the dead poliovirus would "fool" the body into creating antibodies against it without causing the disease itself—a method he had used in his previous research with influenza vaccines. Many others—for example, Dr. Albert Sabin—preferred a vaccine using a live but weakened (or "attenuated") virus, but Salk's vaccine was the first to be tested on groups of humans.

Salk and his team laboriously identified three distinct types of the poliovirus. They realized they would have to create a vaccine that successfully protected against them all. Large quantities of the poliovirus were grown "in vitro" (that is, in cells removed from the living organism from which they came), using cultures of monkey kidney tissue. The goal of Salk's team was to inactivate the virus with just the right amount of formaldehyde to make the virus noninfectious but still able to stimulate the production of protective antibodies. Eventually they created a vaccine (made up of the three strains of the inactivated poliovirus) that did just that.

The first tests on small groups of humans were conducted by Salk's team in the summer of 1952. The researchers also eventually vaccinated themselves and family members. Some of these early subjects already had polio. They were given a vaccine matching the strain of polio already in their system in order to test whether even higher antibody levels could be stimulated. (In my story, I imagined that Franny might have heard about these particular tests with polio victims, misunderstanding the intent of the researchers and imagining a "cure.") No one contracted the disease after receiving the vaccine during these small initial experiments, and it was determined by means of blood tests that the vaccination produced protective antibodies.

On March 26, 1953, on a CBS radio program entitled *The Scientist Speaks for Himself*, largely to calm the nation and ask for patience, Salk announced that an effective, safe vaccine had been tested on small groups of human subjects. In May 1953 and in the early months of 1954, Salk and his team initiated the first community-based pilot trials of the vaccine, inoculating thousands of Pittsburgh schoolchildren. And on April 26, 1954, the largest controlled vaccine field trial in the history of medicine began. It involved 1.8 million grade-school children at 217 test sites in 44 states, and more than 300,000 doctors, teachers, nurses, and volunteers helped administer the vaccine. A year later, on April 12, 1955, the statistical results were announced based on a study of those who had received the vaccine compared with those who had received a placebo (an inert inoculation) or no vaccination at all. Headlines across the world proclaimed, "The Vaccine Works!" Those who had, relatively recently, rejoiced at the end of World War II now rejoiced at the end of another war: the war against polio. Jonas Salk was hailed as a hero and a savior.

The character Francine B. Katzenback is based on stories and memoirs of those stricken by polio during that time. Each person's story was unique; however, many shared certain aspects. Like Franny, some people were visited by "angels," who were actually white-clad nurses ministering to them during their fevers. Many remembered the isolation they endured because of others' ignorance, prejudice, and fear. For this reason, and because of the physical inaccessibility of many municipal buildings, the disabled children were often prevented from attending school with their friends. Creswell School is fictional, but there was a Memorial Home for Crippled Children in Squirrel Hill, now the Children's Institute. Franny makes a rebellious statement at the end of my story, but in real life she probably would have been required to continue her education at the Home, which was, and still is, an excellent institution.

Caregivers ran the gamut from saintly to mean, as I've depicted. Frightened parents were dependent upon the advice of "experts." Sometimes, patients' limbs were treated by casting and splinting in an attempt to restore normal alignment. The method of treating polio developed by Sister Elizabeth Kenny, an Australian bush nurse and former British army nurse—hence, the honorific title "Sister" (she was not a nun)—was a godsend to patients. Her technique involved applying hot, wet packs of wool to relax contracted muscles, followed by stretching of the paralyzed limbs by the caregiver. In a 1951 Gallup poll, Americans considered her the most admirable woman in the world. However, some caregivers' abuse and lack of compassion greatly aggravated the situation for those in their care. Since wheelchairs were very often viewed as restrictive and cumbersome, the ultimate goal was to help the patient walk again, even if "walking" entailed crutches, braces, and an unwieldy gait.

There are several silver linings threaded through the story of polio in America. These include the miraculous advances in research, disease prevention, and public-health efforts the crisis stimulated. Organized voluntarism became a strong part of our national consciousness as well. Although the *Pittsburgh Rag* is fictional, the other newspaper clippings in the story are based on actual articles of the time from the *Pittsburgh Press* and the *Pittsburgh Post-Gazette,* reflecting the pride and community spirit of that city. Towns and cities across America replicated that spirit with an outpouring of funds, time, and energy devoted to the polio campaign. Dr. Salk himself was known to wonder why this energy and commitment could not be applied to all our community problems.

Another silver lining, and the one most relevant to Franny's story, is that the community spirit didn't end when the disease was eradicated in North America. In a way, it represented the beginning of an important part of American history. Many polio victims grew up to fight for the rights of the disabled, especially when they entered college or university in the turbulent 1960s, adding their voices to those of other disabled persons—indeed, all those struggling for basic civil rights. I like to imagine that Franny would have been one of those protestors.

The disabled had never before been perceived as having "rights"; they were simply expected to adjust to the needs and wishes of the rest of society. Mobility, job equality, and inclusion in public education were often denied them; physical accommodations—such as curb cuts, wheelchair ramps, and parking spots and bathroom facilities for the handicapped—did not yet exist. Their protests and demands led to the passage of the Education of All Handicapped Children Act in 1975 (known today as the Individuals with Disabilities Education Act), the Americans with Disabilities Act of 1990, and other civil rights achievements. Though much work remains to be done, today's society better accommodates the needs of the disabled and recognizes that the wheelchair, which once carried such a stigma, can be both liberating and empowering.

The outreach efforts of worldwide organizations have eradicated polio almost everywhere. However, the disease still exists in some underdeveloped countries. Often, irrational fears and unfounded rumors about the polio vaccine prevent children from receiving it. There is no cure for polio, but it can be prevented, and those who remain unvaccinated may still be infectious to others, even if they themselves show no signs of the disease.

It is often difficult for us in the twenty-first century to imagine a time when vaccines for dreaded diseases did not exist. Researchers at the University of Pittsburgh, in an analysis of fifty-six diseases going back to the nineteenth century, have concluded that childhood vaccinations have prevented more than a hundred million cases of contagious disease in the United States alone since 1924.

To many, Franz Kafka's stories reflect the meaningless and unpredictability of life, and certainly Franny's life seems to take a Kafkaesque turn. Yet sometimes literature, and life itself, offers hidden beauties. The professor arrives at an understanding of Kafka's *The Metamorphosis*, inspired by Franny's self-acceptance and endurance.

Zadie Ben's story about the "broken vessels" and the light trapped within their broken shards is attributed to Rabbi Isaac Luria in the sixteenth century. The story represents an important aspect of Jewish tradition called *tikkun olam*, or "the healing of the world," which many define as repair through social action. The "light" can be taken to mean tolerance, justice, and peace, all the good stuff meant to be delivered to the world in that vessel, and which every one of us can help release from those metaphorical shards. I very much wanted to write a story about a young girl disabled by polio who begins to repair the world in her small way.

I also wanted to write about someone who is able to find great solace in books, good people, the delights of the imagination, and the power of her own voice. That's Franny, and, if we are as fortunate as she, that's all of us.

BIBLIOGRAPHY

ON A SPECIAL SHELF IN THE AUTHOR'S BOOKCASE, SOME OF THE CHILDREN'S BOOKS BELOVED BY FRANNY

Alcott, Louisa May. *Little Women*. New York: Grosset & Dunlap, 1947.

Barrie, J. M. *Peter Pan*. New York: Puffin Books, 2010.

Baum, L. Frank. *The Wonderful Wizard of Oz*. 100th anniversary edition. New York: HarperCollins, 2000.

Burnett, Frances Hodgson. *The Secret Garden*. 100th anniversary edition. New York: HarperCollins, 2011.

Carroll, Lewis. *Alice's Adventures in Wonderland*. New York: Puffin Books, 2008.

Farley, Walter. *The Black Stallion*. New York: Random House, 1971.

Montgomery, L. M. *Anne of Green Gables*. Toronto, Ontario: Ryerson Press, 1955.

O'Hara, Mary. *My Friend Flicka*. New York: HarperFestival, 2003.

Sewell, Anna. *Black Beauty*. London, England: Vintage Random House, 2012.

Steinbeck, John. *The Red Pony*. New York: Penguin Books, 1994.

Stevenson, Robert Louis. *Treasure Island*. New York: Dover, 1993.

White, E. B. *Charlotte's Web*. Illustrated by Garth Williams. New York: HarperTrophy, 1980.

Wilder, Laura Ingalls. *Little House in the Big Woods*. Illustrated by Garth Williams. New York: HarperCollins, 2004.

ON OTHER SHELVES

Beisser, Arnold. *Flying Without Wings: Personal Reflections on Loss, Disability, and Healing*. New York: Bantam, 1990.

De Kruif, Paul. *Microbe Hunters*. New York: Harcourt, 1926.

Dillard, Annie. *An American Childhood*. New York: Harper Perennial, 2008.

Fleischer, Doris Zames, and Frieda Zames. *The Disability Rights Movement: From Charity to Confrontation.* 2nd ed. Philadelphia: Temple University Press, 2011.

Gould, Tony. *A Summer Plague: Polio and Its Survivors.* New Haven: Yale University Press, 1995.

Gray, William S., A. Sterl Artley, and May Hill Arbuthnot. *The New We Look and See.* 1st ed. Illustrated by Eleanor Campbell. New York: Scott Foresman and Company, 1951.

Greenblatt, Stephen. *The Swerve: How the World Became Modern.* New York: Norton, 2011.

Heumann, Judith E. *Disability Rights and Independent Living Movement Oral History Project: Pioneering Disability Rights Advocate and Leader in Disabled in Action, New York; Center for Independent Living, Berkeley; World Institute on Disability; and the US Department of Education, 1960s–2000.* Online Archive of California, 2004.

Kehret, Peg. *Small Steps: The Year I Got Polio.* Anniversary edition. Morton Grove, Ill.: Albert Whitman & Co., 2006.

Mattlin, Ben. *Miracle Boy Grows Up: How the Disability Rights Revolution Saved My Sanity.* New York: Skyhorse, 2012.

McCormick, Adele von Rüst, and Marlena Deborah McCormick. *Horse Sense and the Human Heart: What Horses Can Teach Us About Trust, Bonding, Creativity and Spirituality.* Deerfield Beach, Fla.: Health Communications, 1997.

Neumayer, Peter F. *The Annotated Charlotte's Web.* New York: HarperCollins, 1994.

Nichols, Janice Flood. *Twin Voices: A Memoir of Polio, the Forgotten Killer.* Bloomington, Ind.: iUniverse, 2008.

Oshinsky, David M. *Polio: An American Story.* New York: Oxford University Press, 2005.

Rogers, Naomi. *Polio Wars: Sister Kenny and the Golden Age of American Medicine.* New York: Oxford University Press, 2014.

Sass, Edmund J., with George Gottfried and Anthony Sorem. *Polio's Legacy: An Oral History*. Lanham, Md.: University Press of America, 1996.

Scott, Naomi. *Special Needs, Special Horses: A Guide to the Benefits of Therapeutic Riding*. Denton: University of North Texas Press, 2005.

Seavey, Nina Gilden, Jane S. Smith, and Paul Wagner. *A Paralyzing Fear: The Triumph Over Polio in America*. New York: TV Books, 1998.

Shapiro, Joseph P. *No Pity: People with Disabilities Forging a New Civil Rights Movement*. New York: Three Rivers Press, 1994.

Silver, Julie, and Daniel Wilson. *Polio Voices: An Oral History from the American Polio Epidemics and Worldwide Eradication Efforts*. Westport, Conn.: Praeger, 2007.

Squirrel Hill Historical Society. *Images of America: Squirrel Hill*. Charleston, S.C.: Arcadia, 2005.

van Panhuis, Willem G., and others. "Contagious Diseases in the U.S. from 1988 to the Present." *New England Journal of Medicine*, 2013; 369:2152–58, November 28, 2013.

Vaughan, Roger. *Listen to the Music: The Life of Hilary Koprowski*. New York: Springer-Verlag, 2000.

Wilson, Daniel J. *Living with Polio: The Epidemic and Its Survivors*. Chicago: University of Chicago Press, 2005.

OTHER RESOURCES

Pittsburgh Press archives
Pittsburgh Post-Gazette archives

Timeline Development of the Salk Polio Vaccine at the University of Pittsburgh:
http://www.salk.edu/about/discovery_timeline.html

Film about Salk and the Vaccine:
http://www.shotfeltroundtheworld.com/index.php

Videos by Students:
http://www.takeashotcontest.org/polio-entries

The Bill and Melinda Gates Foundation and Polio Partners:
http://www.gatesfoundation.org/What-We-Do/Global-Development/Polio/
Partners

Post-Polio Health International:
www.polioplace.org; www.post-polio.org; www.ventusers.org

An annotated list of some of the writers, composers, musicians, entertainers,
and celebrities appreciated by Fleabrain and Franny:
www.joannerocklin.com

SONGS

"A Dream Is a Wish Your Heart Makes," written and composed by Mack
David, Al Hoffman, and Jerry Livingston for the Walt Disney movie
Cinderella, 1950.

"Happy Birthday to You," the melody allegedly from the song "Good Morning
to All," by American siblings Patty and Mildred J. Hill, 1893.

"Heigh-Ho," by Frank Churchill (music) and Larry Morey (lyrics) for the Walt
Disney movie *Snow White and the Seven Dwarfs*, 1937.

"It Ain't Gonna Rain No Mo'" by Wendell Woods Hall, 1923.

"Three Little Words" by Harry Ruby (music) and Burt Kalmar (lyrics), 1930.

"Too Young," by Sidney Lippman (music) and Sylvia Dee (lyrics) in 1951, sung
by Nat King Cole in the same year.

"Yankee Doodle," an Anglo-American song dating back to the Seven Years'
War (1756–63).

ACKNOWLEDGMENTS

It has been a joy discovering the Wonders of Pittsburgh, past and present, aided by current and former Pittsburghers generous with memories of their beloved city (and in particular, Squirrel Hill): Gary Apter, Fern Bathhurst, Gerry Buncher, Barbara Friedland, Susan Klee, Linda Marcus, Jerry Perlmutter, and Vera Weiss. And for their above-and-beyond generosity and boundless patience, special thank-yous to Abbot Friedland, Audrey Glickman of the Squirrel Hill Historical Society, Elva Perrin, Nanci Perrin, Michelle Pilecki, and Mel Solomon. Thank you as well to Art Louderback, Head Librarian, Thomas and Katherine Detre Library and Archives, Senator John Heinz History Center, Pittsburgh, and David R. Grinnell, Reference and Access Archivist, Archives Service Center, University of Pittsburgh Library System.

I am also indebted to Izi Kulkin, Deb Rodriguez, and Harriet Sturtz for their special expertise, as well as the wise input from Joan Headley, Director of Post-Polio International.

My talented critique group helped me unfold the core of my story: Diane Fraser, Suzi Jensen, Marissa Moss, Emily Polsby, and Eleanor Vincent. And, as always, I am grateful for the support and guidance of my agent Erin Murphy, and all of her team at the Erin Murphy Literary Agency, as well as my editor Maggie Lehrman and the hardworking team at Abrams.

All my love and gratitude to my wonderful family who keep me in touch with what is true and important, so I can go down to my basement and into my head and try to write about it.

Q&A WITH JOANNE ROCKLIN

Each reader will have his or her own answers.
Joanne Rocklin has provided hers to start the conversation.

Is Fleabrain real?

Joanne Rocklin: Yes, Fleabrain is real, just as Charlotte is real, as are the heroic mice and wizards and sundry talented characters in other books. That is, the characters are real within the context and power of the story. But perhaps you are asking whether Franny and Fern are imagining the powers of Fleabrain and Charlotte in order to better accept, or occasionally escape from, some difficult facts of life. That conclusion is certainly possible. But I would wager that fantasy characters are very, very real to the authors as they write. I myself often wonder what Fleabrain would think or say about this or that . . .

Why do Fleabrain and Franny and Professor Doctor Gutman each reflect on Kafka's Die Verwandlung (known in English as The Metamorphosis)?

JR: Many readers have pondered Kafka's mysterious story about a man who changes into a giant bug overnight. Fleabrain is intrigued because it's a tale about a fellow insect. He knows that Kafka is a famous author and that he should understand his work. Franny knows what it's like to be transformed and then shunned by others. She is entranced by the book's scary cover and the fact that people seem to think that Kafka has all the answers. The professor finally arrives at his own understanding of Kafka's story, and of life itself, inspired by Franny's self-acceptance and endurance.

Franny loves E. B. White's *Charlotte's Web*. How do Fleabrain's "three words" compare with the words Charlotte weaves for Wilbur the pig?

JR: Charlotte is wiser and more mature than Fleabrain. Her woven words always lead to what is best for Wilbur—namely, a decrease in his loneliness, an increase in his self-esteem and joyfulness, and an escape from death by hatchet. Fleabrain's final three words show how much he himself has finally learned about friendship and life. His words selflessly encourage Franny to focus on changing her own world, with the help of other loved ones who may know as much as, or more than, he.

Fleabrain and Franny often refer to "smallness." How is this concept important to the story?

JR: Franny feels small and helpless in the face of her illness, like a little bird with a broken wing. Everyone else seems to know what's best for her. Fleabrain is small, yet he feels smart and powerful. Because of their friendship, Franny begins to feel that way, too. They both understand that there are invisible tiny things (viruses, atoms, aspects of our DNA) that are very powerful, for both good and bad. And they discover that sometimes it's our small, daily actions that lead to big changes: speaking the truth, being a good friend, practicing the clarinet, doggedly researching a scientific dilemma.

What does it mean to "free the light from the broken shards"?

JR: Zadie tells Franny an ancient, mystical story about a giant vessel that contained all the light needed to create a perfect world. When the vessel exploded, the light was pierced by the shards and trapped within them. What kind of light can create a perfect world? Zadie, Franny, Fleabrain, and I all believe that this "light" represents tolerance, justice, peace, civil rights, and more: all the good stuff meant to be delivered to the world, that each one of us can help release from those metaphorical shards.

ABOUT THE AUTHOR

Joanne Rocklin is the author of *One Day and One Amazing Morning on Orange Street*, which won the California Library Association's John and Patricia Beatty Award, and *The Five Lives of Our Cat Zook*, which won the Golden Kite Award for fiction from the Society of Children's Book Writers and Illustrators and a Parents' Choice Gold Award. She lives in Oakland, California.